TRAPPED
IN
HITLER'S
WEB

Also by Marsha Forchuk Skrypuch

Making Bombs for Hitler
The War Below
Stolen Girl
Don't Tell the Nazis

TRAPPED IN HITLER'S WEB

A novel by
MARSHA FORCHUK SKRYPUCH

SCHOLASTIC INC.

FOR TUSIO, MUSIA, OREST, AND ROMAN

All rights reserved. Published by Scholastic Inc., *Publishers since 1920.* SCHOLASTIC and associated logos are trademarks and/or registered trademarks of Scholastic Inc.

The publisher does not have any control over and does not assume any responsibility for author or third-party websites or their content.

While inspired by real events and historical characters, this is a work of fiction and does not claim to be historically accurate or portray factual events or relationships. Please keep in mind that references to actual persons, living or dead, business establishments, events, or locales may not be factually accurate but rather fictionalized by the author.

Library of Congress Cataloging-in-Publication Data available

ISBN 978-1-338-67259-6

10 9 8 7 6 5 4 3 2 1   20 21 22 23 24

Printed in the U.S.A.   40

First printing 2020

Book design by Yaffa Jaskoll

CHAPTER ONE
HIDING IN PLAIN SIGHT

October 1942, Nazi–Occupied Lviv, Ukraine

I stood beside Nathan and stared at the ad plastered on the wall outside the Reich Employment Office. The poster urged Ukrainians to sign up for work in the Reich. The Germans would feed us, pay us, and give us free time on Sundays. It seemed almost too good to be true.

"We *have* to do it," whispered Nathan, squeezing my hand. "I've got Bohdan's identity papers. I'll be safe."

What choice did we have? If we stayed in the woods much longer, we'd freeze to death. But we couldn't go back to our homes in Viteretz, not while the Nazis were killing Jews. It had started slowly, after the Germans occupied our town. Nathan was Jewish. And even though he was now passing himself off as Bohdan Sawchuk, everyone in Viteretz knew that the real Bohdan had been killed by the

1

Soviets. And what would the cruel German Commandant do to me, Mama, and my big sister, Krystia, for helping Nathan survive? No. We couldn't return there.

Mama and Krystia.

Just the thought of them made my heart ache. I longed to be home again, to snuggle up at night together, to share a story over a bowl of warm kasha. Poor Mama would have so much work to do without me there to help her. I even missed arguing with Krystia. Was she happy that she now got our bed all to herself? The sooner this war ended, the better, and then we could all get back to a normal life.

But right now, I had to help Nathan stay alive.

We had to hide, but Nathan's false papers would only work if we didn't draw any attention to ourselves.

Two Ukrainians going to the Reich for work would seem like a normal choice—even a good one—to a Nazi. Could going into the heart of Hitler's Reich be our salvation? I hoped and prayed that our plan to hide in plain sight would work.

So here we stood, wearing everything we owned. I had on my threadbare skirt and blouse plus the oversized jacket and boots that my Auntie Iryna had given me during the short time we were in hiding with the help of the Underground; my hair was in one long braid down my back. Nathan had escaped the Nazis with nothing but his underwear. When he came to our house to beg me, Mama, and Krystia for refuge, we had dressed him in clothing from our relatives who had already been killed in the war—mostly Uncle Roman's, but some from cousin Josip as well. In our pockets were some coins paid to us in the back streets of Lviv in exchange for things foraged from the woods—mushrooms, nuts, and berries.

How I wished I were as brave as Krystia. She wouldn't hesitate, but would just plunge ahead in spite of danger. I straightened my spine and pretended I was her. I marched up the stone steps, pulled the door open, and stepped inside, Nathan beside me.

A few people stood in line and we got in behind them. The officer at the desk looked at both of our passports side by side. "You're young to be going to Germany," he said. "But you look healthy and I won't argue."

He filled out a form and handed it to me. As he worked on Nathan's form, I held my breath, worried that he'd realize that Nathan wasn't Bohdan Sawchuk. But he completed it with the same ease as mine and handed it back.

"Take these to her," he said, pointing to a woman with a typewriter at the far end of the room. "She'll make up your official work documents."

As we waited our turn in front of the typist's desk, I examined the officer's handwritten form and realized with a sinking heart that I had been assigned to a metalworks factory, which would be hard work even for an adult. Nathan's assignment was the same as mine. A hard fate, yes, but better than staying in Viteretz. We'd be paid and fed and have a warm place to sleep, which was more than we'd had for months.

The person in front of us finished, and I was now face-to-face with the typist, her dark blond hair coiled on top of her head and a pair of severe black glasses perched on the tip of her nose. I handed her my paper.

"You're not from Lemberg but from Liebhaft, I see," she said, using the new German names for Lviv and Viteretz as she smoothed the form out on her desk. "You've volunteered, and you're just eleven years old," she said in a lower voice, almost to herself.

"I'll be twelve in two months." The words burst out against my will.

She inserted a card into the typewriter and keyed in the words from the form, but she paused partway through. She slid open the top drawer of her desk and appeared to be looking at something in there before keying in more information. When she was finished, she pulled the card out of the typewriter carriage and set it on the desk in front of me. With her other hand, she flipped open a metal container, revealing a dark blue square.

"Put your index finger on this ink pad," she said. "And then place your inky finger on this spot."

I did as she said. She picked up the new document and waved it to dry the ink of my fingerprint. As she handed it back to me, her firm expression briefly flickered into a smile.

She took Nathan's passport next. She put her finger on the year of his birth, and for a moment I nearly panicked. But then she looked up at him and said, "You're a young one too. Just twelve and volunteering to go to the Reich for work." Her tone sounded almost sympathetic.

I held my breath as she prepared Nathan's papers, hoping and praying that his false identity would pass scrutiny. I exhaled in relief when she finished typing up his card and had him make a fingerprint just as I had done.

"You need to be at the train station by noon today," she said. "Pack enough food for a two-day journey. I'm glad to see that you've both got shoes and a warm jacket. You'll need them."

CHAPTER TWO
NICOLETTA

I didn't realize just how scared I was until we got back out onto the street. I bent over, clutching my waist, heaving. I felt like I was about to throw up.

"It's okay," said Nathan, rubbing my back. "We've got our cards."

These work cards were like gold. As far as the Nazis were concerned, having them proved we weren't runaways. More important, Nathan's was proof he wasn't Jewish.

I stood up straight and filled my lungs with cool air, trying to calm myself. "Let's hope we did the right thing."

"Just think," Nathan said as he took his coins out of his pocket. "Soon, we'll be making money. We should send this home."

Was it possible? And who was still alive back home? We'd hidden from the Nazis with the Underground for just a few days last spring and then struck out on our own.

Every once in a while over the summer months, we'd made contact with them. In July we'd heard that Mr. Segal, Nathan's father, was still alive, and my mother and sister were too. That was the last we heard. I looked up to see the time on the City Hall clock tower. It was ten a.m., two hours until the train.

"Come with me," I said, my hand on Nathan's elbow.

We weaved our way through the backstreets of Lviv to a place that I knew only from Auntie Iryna's careful description. I led Nathan through an alleyway behind a street of stores and a restaurant. Between two metal cans piled high with rank and rotting food was a door marked BISTRO MYKOLA—DELIVERIES ONLY.

I tapped on it. No answer.

"What are we doing here?" asked Nathan.

"The owner knows Auntie Iryna," I said. "And I'm hoping she'll send a message back home for us." Auntie Iryna had described this woman's appearance in detail and I could only hope that I'd recognize her on sight.

I tapped more firmly on the door, but there was still no answer.

"Are you sure it's even locked?" asked Nathan. He pulled on the handle. It opened.

We stepped inside, and I called out, "Hello, is anybody here?"

A woman appeared, looking flustered. "We have no food for beggars," she said, trying to shove us back out the door and close it in our faces.

She was in her twenties, with dark eyes and silver-framed oval glasses and light hair in braids, just as Auntie had described. This woman was definitely Auntie's friend.

"You are Nicoletta Tokarowetz," I said. "And I'm Maria Fediuk, Iryna Fediuk's niece."

The woman's eyebrows rose in surprise.

She didn't look convinced. Since she was working with the Underground, she'd expect me to know the code words, but we hadn't had contact with the Underground for a while and the code words were constantly changing. I did know the pattern though. When we were staying with the Underground, we had been cycling through classic quotes from Ukrainian poets, so maybe a quote from a poet at the end of the alphabet would get the point across.

"I haven't seen a *falcon* for some months now," I told her, "falcon" being our local code word for the Underground Army. "But I have a heart that does not die."

"From the hands of death?" she asked.

"Immortality," I answered.

She nodded. "Not the most current, but it will do."

Nathan looked from me to Nicoletta.

"Quotes from Lesia Ukrainka," I told him.

"Who's your friend?" she asked.

"I'm Bohdan Sawchuk," he said, stepping forward and bowing slightly.

"Bohdan Sawchuk of Viteretz?" Nicoletta asked. "The same Bohdan who was executed by the Soviets in June 1941? Who are you *really*?"

His face paled, and at first, he didn't answer but looked between me and Nicoletta and reconsidered. "I'm Nathan Segal," he said.

"The photographer's son?" asked Nicoletta.

"Yes."

"He's still supplying photographs for the false papers." Nathan gripped Nicoletta's hands. "So he's alive?"

"As of last week, yes. That's when our network last got a batch of photos from the ghetto."

"Have you heard anything about Krystia or Mama?" I asked.

"Both still alive," said Nicoletta. "Both still working with us."

My knees felt weak with relief from the news and I might have fallen if Nathan hadn't grabbed my elbow to steady me.

"Come and rest for a minute," said Nicoletta. She ushered us both through the steamy kitchen to a table close by the sink. We sat down, and Nicoletta poured tea. She dropped a lump of sugar in each of our cups and set a thin vanilla cookie on our saucers. Everything about this was a treat. We hadn't been able to make a fire in the woods in case we were caught, so we hadn't had anything hot to eat or drink in months. I hadn't seen sugar in a very long time. And a cookie? I felt like I was dreaming.

"Black market. Only the best will do for my Nazi clientele," Nicoletta said with a bitter edge. "Now tell me why you're here."

"Can you get a message to Auntie Iryna?" I asked.

She nodded.

I took out my work card and set it on the table. "We're going to the Reich," I said. "We want our parents to know how to find us when the war ends."

Nicoletta examined my work card. "How fortunate you are," she said. "You've been given farmwork in the Austrian Alps—far away from the fighting."

"What?" I pulled the card back. She was right. "The officer assigned me to a metalworks factory in Germany," I said. "The typist must have switched it."

Nathan took his card out. "Mine now says farmwork too. At the Huber farm in Thaur, Ostmark."

"Ostmark is the Nazi name for Austria," said Nicoletta. "That's where Maria has also been assigned. That typist is a very good person." She slid the cards back across the table. "I've overheard my German customers talk about evacuating their wives and children to that region for safety. I can't think of a better place for you to be."

I clutched my work card in my hands. Could we really have such good luck? I said a silent prayer of thanks to that typist.

"When does your train leave?" asked Nicoletta.

"At noon," said Nathan.

"We'd better hurry, then," she said, glancing at a clock on the wall. She got up from the table and came back with a pen and paper. Nathan couldn't risk writing directly to his father in case the letter got into Nazi hands, but I wrote my note:

Mama, don't worry. Assigned to the Huber farm near Thaur in Austria. I've heard it's not a bad place. N sends love to father. Will write when we can. Love, M.

From my pocket, I pulled out my coins.

"Here," said Nathan, emptying his pockets. "Send these as well."

I was about to put the coins in the envelope when Nicoletta took them from me. She went to her cash drawer and changed them for a twenty zloty note. "Coins are bulky. Makes it harder to hide the envelope." She sealed the note and the paper money into the envelope and put it into her pocket.

"Thank you for delivering our letter," I said. "And thank you for the tea and cookies."

Nicoletta walked us to the back door, and just before we stepped out, she said, "Wait."

Moments later she came back with two wrapped packages. "Cheese and buns," she said, giving one to each of us. "It's not much, but I hope it will get you through your train ride."

"Thank you," we both said, overwhelmed by this generosity from a person we had just met. I shoved mine into my coat pocket, and Nathan did the same.

"Stay safe," said Nicoletta, closing the door.

I heard a scrape of metal—she had remembered to lock the door from the inside this time.

CHAPTER THREE
WITH THE CAPTIVES

When we were a block away from the train station, I could hear the hum of many voices. As we got closer, there were Nazi soldiers keeping control of the crowd. A few had clipboards, and they were sorting people into groups.

Nathan stopped walking and his face went rigid with fear. I put my hand on his elbow and nudged him forward. "Breathe, *Bohdan*," I whispered. "I'll do the talking."

We went up to one of the soldiers, and I showed him our work cards. "We don't know where to go," I said.

The soldier frowned as he examined them, and my heart sank. Was there something off about them? But then he looked up and said, "How nice for you, going to Ostmark, the land of our Führer's birth. Wait over by those tracks." He pointed to an area where two girls who were about our age stood close together. "You'll take the train to Innsbruck, and from there, someone will take you to the farm."

Hitler was born in Austria? And we were supposed to be *safer* there? The thought made me feel sick again.

When we got to the platform, the taller girl glanced our way. She looked tired; her tangled hair was caught up in a rough ponytail, and her clothing looked like it had been slept in. Both girls were wearing thin *postoly*—handmade leather slippers—hardly good protection with winter coming on. It looked like they hadn't planned very well for the trip.

"Good day," I said, holding out my hand.

She took my hand and said, "I'm Myra. This is my little sister, Krystia."

Krystia.

The same name as my own sister. This little girl looked so young. My guess was that she was nine or ten. With a jolt I realized that I had missed my own sister's birthday while we were hiding in the woods. My Krystia was now thirteen. She was growing up and changing and I wasn't there to see it. If I ever got back to Viteretz, would I even recognize her? Mama was growing older too and, as she did, she'd need more help, but I was far away. I quickly brushed away a tear and took a deep breath. I had to be strong, to get through this war, so everything could go back to how it used to be.

"It's good to meet you," said Nathan, nodding at each of the sisters in turn. "I'm Bohdan." He tugged on my elbow, jolting me out of my thoughts.

"Hello," I managed to say. "I'm Maria."

After that, we stood in silence, watching down the empty tracks. I couldn't stop thinking about Krystia and Mama. What were they doing now? Were they angry that I left? Would my letter comfort or confuse them?

"Not very many people seem to be going to Innsbruck," said Nathan.

And it was true. The soldiers ushered people to various platforms, but they hadn't sent anyone else to stand with the four of us. Maybe these two girls were coming to the Huber farm just like we were.

"Myra," I asked. "Have you and your sister been assigned to a farm?"

She looked at me, puzzled. *"Assigned?"*

"On your work cards, what do they say?"

"What do you mean by work cards?" asked Myra.

I was about to pull mine out of my pocket and show her, but Nathan clamped his hand on top of mine so I couldn't. I opened my mouth to protest, but he gave me a look.

"The soldiers captured us on our way to school," said Myra. "Who would work for Hitler on purpose?"

What? Weren't these all volunteers like us? Just before we'd fled from Viteretz, the Nazis had begun putting up posters, advertising work in the Reich. I knew people from our town who had volunteered. Going to the Reich for work was a way to get food, to stay alive. Why weren't people volunteering anymore? Why did they have to be forced?

Were the Austrian Alps really as safe as Nicoletta said?

I looked more carefully at what people were wearing. Many were barefoot, and some were in their nightclothes.

Panic washed over me. Maybe we should have stayed hiding in the woods after all. Would freezing to death in our sleep have been a kinder way to die than whatever lay ahead for us now?

While these worries consumed me, a freight train grumbled to a halt. A guard got off and pulled open one of the boxcar doors, revealing an exhausted group of kids our age crammed together. Most were sitting, but a few stood, and they did not look like volunteers.

Maybe we should just leave? But the guard nudged me with his rifle. "Get in," he said. "All of you."

I stumbled in, trying not to step on anyone. The doors were pulled shut and I heard the screech of a bolt being locked in place from the outside. We were plunged into semidarkness, with the only light coming in from a small grilled window close to the ceiling.

The train jerked forward, and I would have lost my balance if Nathan hadn't grabbed my arm at the last moment. There was no place left for us to sit, so Nathan and I stepped carefully to the back, and we stood side by side, pinned against the wall by the crush of people.

Myra and Krystia were squeezed in front of us, and Myra's tangled ponytail tickled my nose. When the train suddenly slowed, she stumbled and nearly fell.

"Lean on me or grab my arm if you need to," I said.

She turned and looked at me with anxious eyes, then nodded in thanks.

The train rumbled on for hours with all of us crushed together. No one spoke, and it got stuffy and hot. I would have loved to take my coat off but there was nowhere to put it. Besides, there was food in my pocket. What if I lost it?

The rumble of the train comforted me, and it felt good not to be running and hiding. I didn't mind being so hot. It was definitely better than freezing in the woods. I was still savoring the cookie and sweet tea, plus I had food in my pocket. My eyes felt heavy, so I closed them, but upsetting images kept me awake . . .

Nathan and his parents stand at their doorstep. Nazi soldiers prod them with rifles, forcing them away from their home. I hide behind buildings and watch as they're taken to the Viteretz ghetto, that terrible barbed-wire prison where the Nazis put Jews.

Days go by.

The creak of wheels.

I look through the curtain. A wagonload of Jews.

This isn't the first time Jews are being taken from the ghetto into the woods at the edge of town where a freshly dug grave awaits them.

But this time Nathan is on the wagon.

They are all shot. The bullet aimed at Nathan whizzes past him, but as those around him crumple to the ground, he is pulled into the grave with them. The Nazis throw shovelfuls of dirt over the bodies and Nathan is buried alive, surrounded by the corpses of his friends. The soldiers leave, and he crawls out of that grave and comes to us.

We hide him.

But Nathan knows that if he is caught in our house, we will all be killed.

And that's when I make my decision.

To save Nathan, but also to save Mama and Krystia, I leave with him.

I have my own Ukrainian identity papers, and Nathan has the papers of our dead Christian friend.

I took a deep breath, opened my eyes, and looked around. It took me a moment to remember that I was on a train speeding to Austria. Most of the kids were quiet, either lost in their own thoughts or sleeping. Nathan had his eyes closed, and I wondered if he was sleeping standing up. I hoped that those terrible images that jumbled in my brain didn't come to him as well. I hoped that he had a brief chance to shut off all his worries and maybe get some sleep.

Even though I had no idea what our future held, I still felt hopeful. Mama always said to focus on the small things we could change for the good and not dwell on what was out of our power. The one good thing I had been able to do was to help Nathan escape. He would have been killed if we had stayed but he was still alive, so it must have been the right decision. What would the future hold? Hard to know. I'd just follow Mama's advice and not worry about everything else. I closed my eyes and tried to relax, letting my mind wander with the rumble of the train.

The Alps were far away from the War Front. And how could mountains be bombed? Farms grew food. Farms didn't have soldiers. And neither of us was afraid of decent hard work. Everyone would assume that we were both Christian Ukrainians. Nathan could stay safe from the killing squads, hiding in plain sight.

But as the train took me farther from home, my heart ached at the thought of Mama and Krystia. They would be so worried. But even for them, my decision was for the best. Now their small ration of food only had to be shared with two mouths instead of three. The zlotys we sent through Nicoletta would help them a bit, and the note I sent would ease their worry. What if I could send more money home, once I was paid for the farm work? That would make all the difference in the world to them.

The best part of it was that Nathan and I were together, and that he was safe.

Nathan and I had been friends for so long that I couldn't remember a time that I didn't know him. But now it went beyond friendship because, without my help, Nathan could die. It was important for him to play the part of a Christian Ukrainian convincingly. There were a million little things that he still didn't know that could trip him up. Even earlier with Nicoletta, he hadn't recognized the words from Lesia Ukrainka's poetry despite hearing them many times in the summer. He could now recite *Oche Nash* and *Radichya Marie*—the Lord's Prayer and the Hail Mary—in Ukrainian, and he did a decent job quoting Taras Shevchenko, but he was hopeless when it came to keeping track of the saints' name days that every Christian Ukrainian knows.

I had fallen into a sort of trance, so was startled when the train stopped and the door screeched open. A gust of cool air blew through the boxcar, and I breathed in as much of it as I could. I stood on my tiptoes and tried to see over the heads of the people in front of me.

One of the kids closest to the door said, "The sign says we're in Belzec."

Gasps of panic rippled through the crush of passengers. Nathan, now fully awake, clutched my hand.

Rumors about Belzec had filtered through the Underground while we were hiding out with them. The Nazis had apparently changed their method of killing Jews. Instead of taking small groups of Jews at a time on wagons to be shot at the outskirts of town, they'd built regional camps where thousands were murdered all at once.

People were taken by train to these killing camps, and one of these camps was in Belzec.

A soldier stood on the platform in front of our boxcar. "You, you, you . . ." he said, pointing at random to kids who had the misfortune to be closest to the door. He selected about eight people, and then abruptly pushed the doors shut. Moments later, the train started moving again.

Such a wave of relief passed over me. I was grateful for not being chosen, and that Nathan wasn't chosen either. At the same time, it made me feel guilty. What about the ones who had been chosen? What would happen to them now?

Nathan slumped heavily against me. "I'm scared," he said.

"Me too," I said. But I thought of our work cards tucked safely away. They'd protect us.

Nathan was silent, and as the train chugged on, I thought he must have fallen back asleep, but then he whispered, "Do you think this train actually goes to Innsbruck?"

Myra turned. "It does. At least according to the map of the route that was posted on the platform. Belzec was listed on that map as the first stop."

I hadn't noticed the route map. But Myra's comment made me feel a little bit better about our situation. Now that there were fewer people in the boxcar, there was enough room to sit, but we still stayed at the back so we could lean against the wall. I also figured that the farther we stayed from the door, the better. Myra propped herself against my knees and Krystia curled up in her sister's lap and fell asleep.

I was very thirsty, but in the entire boxcar, there was just one open pail of sloshing water with a single dipper. Every few hours the dipper would be passed around and we'd each take a sip. The water had to last: Who knew when the pail would be filled again?

The train chugged on for what seemed like more than a day. I was hungry and could easily have eaten my entire bun with cheese, but I didn't feel that I could take it out and eat it. As far as I could tell, most of the others in our car had been captured. They wouldn't have had time to pack food. How could I eat my bun and cheese with so many other hungry people around?

Finally, I couldn't stand it anymore. Maybe we'd each only have a bite, but I'd share what I had. "Does anyone else have food?" I asked, holding up my bun and cheese.

"I do," said Nathan, holding up his as well.

"So do I," said another boy, who sat close to the front. He held up a small cloth sack. "Dried blueberries," he said.

Someone held up a bottle of soured milk and someone else said, "Here's an apple." Myra took a piece of *kobasa* out of her pocket. "I stole it," she said, looking sheepish. One girl took out a bag of cheese curds and another had one raw onion.

Myra drew out a pocket knife and we divvied up the food as best we could, making sure everyone in the boxcar got at least one bite. My own bite of bread with cheese and a bit of onion tasted heavenly, but it didn't stop the growling hunger in the pit of my stomach.

In addition to our pail of water, there was another sloshing pail close to the door. It had been put in empty at Lviv, and we were using it as our only toilet. As the hours passed and it got fuller, I was gagging at the smell of it. When the train stopped again, and the doors opened, a soldier took the stinky pail out and replaced it with an empty one. He also passed in a pail full of water. I stretched and breathed in as much fresh air as I could.

"We're in Vienna," said the boy who'd contributed dried blueberries.

Just like at Belzec, some of the young people were selected. But instead of doing it randomly, the soldier stepped in and waded through us, hand-selecting those he wanted.

When he stopped in front of me, I stood up obediently, but said, "I think I'm supposed to stay on the train until Innsbruck."

"Why would you think that?" he asked, an amused look on his face.

I dug into my waistband and pulled out my work card. He took it from me and examined it carefully, then said, "You stay on the train."

He held it up high and said, "Anyone else have one of these?"

Silence in response, then Nathan said, "I have one."

The soldier handed the card back to me and I put it in my pocket. He examined Nathan's, then handed it back. "You two stay on the train until Innsbruck," he said.

He turned and pointed to Myra. "You come with me."

My heart sank. Myra would have been safe if they'd taken me, but now she was leaving. As she stood, she didn't look my way. Next, the soldier selected Krystia. I tried to wave good-bye as they filed out behind the soldier, but neither girl turned.

I felt awful. If we hadn't had work cards, those two girls would still be sitting on the train, going toward the Alps and safety. As the doors closed and the train chugged away, I slid down to the floor and wept. Nathan knelt beside me and put a hand on my shoulder. "Maybe they'll be fine," he said. "We have no way of knowing whether getting off here is worse than staying until Innsbruck."

Nathan was right; we couldn't know what would happen to them, and didn't Germans evacuate their own children to Vienna? It had to be safer, the farther we got away from the Front. We had been crushed together for more than a day and I had become used to Myra's weight on my knees and the comforting sound of Krystia as she slept. And then in a flash, they were gone.

I said a silent prayer, hoping they would be able to stay together and be safe. And then I said another prayer of thanks to that typist in Lviv. Why had she chosen to take pity on me and Nathan? Was it because we were young? Or maybe she knew people in Viteretz? Or maybe, as Nicoletta said, she was a good person.

At Salzburg, more young people were herded off, and just as at the other stops, soldiers waded in, not asking for work cards, but just picking people at random. One of the soldiers pointed to Nathan, saying, "You look like a good strong boy."

Nathan scrambled to his feet, then handed his work card to the soldier. "I've been told to stay on the train until Innsbruck."

The soldier looked at his card, but instead of giving it back, he put it in his pocket. "Your assignment can be changed. I need a strong boy. This farmer is just going to have to do without you."

"But . . ." said Nathan.

The soldier ignored his protests. He grabbed Nathan by the arm and escorted him off the train.

I scrambled to my feet and followed them. "I volunteer to come with you," I shouted.

Nathan looked at me, his face pale, but in a firm voice he said, "Get back on the train right now, Maria. I need you to be safe."

The soldier turned. "We're taking boys here, not girls." He grabbed me by the shoulders and pushed me backward onto the train. My tailbone hit the boxcar floor and my skull smacked into a fellow prisoner's kneecap. I was momentarily stunned.

I blinked twice and caught one last glimpse of Nathan's face, and then the doors slammed shut.

CHAPTER FOUR
ALONE

All our careful planning, all our good luck—it had vanished in a flash. I wrapped my arms around my knees and curled into a ball. All I could do was weep.

How could I survive without Nathan by my side? And how would he survive without me? What if they found out he was Jewish? He still didn't know all the tricks to get by.

My big sister had always teased me about being timid, and she was right. I had always leaned on someone else, whether it was her, Mama, or Nathan. I couldn't imagine life without one of them. But here I was, alone for the first time in my life, traveling into the country where Hitler was born.

How would Nathan manage? How would I? Would I ever see Mama or Krystia again? Of all the stupid mistakes I had ever made in my life, this had to be the worst, thinking that somehow traveling into the Reich would be safer than staying at home.

I was so wrapped up in grief and regret that I barely noticed when the train shuddered to yet another stop.

It was in the wee hours of the morning, and most of the kids were sleeping. When the door slid open, streetlamps lit up our boxcar. Soldiers came in just as they had at the other stops and began shaking people at random to wake them up.

The girl who had shared her soured milk said, "We're in Innsbruck."

I now thought of my work card as a curse. Should I even get off here? Maybe I could just stay on the train until it turned around and went back to Lviv. Maybe it would be possible to go back home.

But a soldier stepped inside and pointed to me. "Get up," he said. "Everyone is getting off here."

I stumbled to my feet and followed the soldier out to the platform. There were about twelve of us left. As my eyes got used to the light from the streetlamps, I noticed a few men in civilian overcoats who stood off to one side, each holding a sheaf of papers. None of these men looked like farmers.

When the boxcar doors were closed, and the train had left the station, one of the soldiers went up to the businessmen.

"What do you need?" the soldier asked a thin bearded man in a dark green wool overcoat.

"Three for my quarry," said the man.

"Take your pick."

The man came over to our group and looked us over one by one, then pointed at me and two boys.

"I'm supposed to go to the Huber farm," I said, showing the soldier my card.

"Sit over there," said the soldier, pointing to a bench under the street lamp.

The quarry man picked another girl in my place and then they left. I watched as the rest of the kids got divvied up among the businessmen. One went to road work, one to a bakery, but the rest went to a munitions plant.

It was too dark to see exactly where all the captives were being taken, but those for the munitions plant got into the back of a tarp-covered truck.

When everyone else was gone, the soldier took me to a warehouse about a block away from the train station. "The farmer will get you in the morning," he said, pausing in front of a warehouse door. "Meanwhile, you'll have to stay here." He unbolted the door, opened it, and flicked a switch. A bare bulb dangling from a wire dimly illuminated metal shelves and a concrete floor. I stepped in and he closed the door behind me. I could hear him slide the metal bolt into place. I was locked in.

He hadn't left food or water and I was utterly alone. I was filled with worry and fear, but I was also dead tired. There was nothing I would have liked more than to crawl into my own bed at home and snuggle in beside my big sister. I would pull the comforter up to my neck and fall asleep, Krystia's warmth making me feel safe and cozy. Even though I could barely stay awake, I didn't want to lie on the cold concrete floor. I didn't want to sit either: My muscles were stiff and sore from too much sitting. I paced slowly from one end of the room to the other, then turned around and did it again. As I walked, my legs loosened up, but it didn't make me feel any better about my situation. How could I have been so stupid to think that going into the Reich for work was the way to protect Nathan from the Nazis? Now he was in Salzburg without me. How long would it take until they figured out he was Jewish? And then there was Mama and Krystia. I had messed up everything, making it worse for everyone I loved.

I paced and paced and paced and paced. What was happening to Nathan? I could only pray that whatever job they wanted boys to do in Salzburg was a safe one.

I paced and waited for my farmer to arrive.

CHAPTER FIVE
COW STALLS

Innsbruck, Austria

Hours later, the screech of the metal bolt startled me from my thoughts. The door opened, and sunlight poured in. I was so grateful to see that it wasn't a soldier or a business-man standing there, but a grizzled farmer in a soft felt hat and leather trousers held up by suspenders.

He blinked a few times, then peered over my shoulder. "Where are the rest of them?" he asked.

"It's just me."

He pulled a paper from the back pocket of his trou-sers and unfolded it. "Says here we're getting eight foreign workers." He looked at me sternly. "Did the rest of them escape?"

"I don't know anything about eight workers, Herr Huber," I said in as polite a voice as I could manage. "I was traveling with just one other worker assigned to your farm, but the soldiers took him off at Salzburg."

"Again? Those darned bridge builders," he muttered. "They must have bribed someone. How does Hitler expect us to feed our troops if he won't give us workers?"

Bridge building. That sounded like a hard and dangerous job. Was Nathan strong enough to build a bridge? And what would happen to him if he wasn't?

The man startled me from my worries. "Show me your work card."

"Here it is, Herr Huber," I said, taking it from my waistband.

"I am not Herr Huber," said the man, taking my card and examining it carefully. "Now show me your passport."

My heart sank.

Not Herr Huber? The last piece of our careful plan had just crumbled away. What would happen to me now?

I opened my passport to show him. The man took it and put it in his own shirt pocket along with my work card.

I gasped. I felt naked without my papers.

"You're so scrawny, and just a girl, but I guess you're better than nothing." The farmer stepped out of the barn and motioned for me to follow.

I had to follow him. My identity was his hostage, and so was I.

As my eyes adjusted to the broad daylight, the first thing I saw was a large dog with a drooling tongue bounding toward me. I hid behind the man for protection.

"Please don't let it hurt me!" I screamed.

"Max, sit," the man said sternly to the dog. And it obeyed him!

He took me by the shoulders and walked me up to the dog. "Give Max your hand to sniff," he said. "He needs to know that you're a friend."

Around Viteretz, we would see wild dogs now and then, but you'd never go up to one and hold out your hand. Some of the Nazi officers had dogs so fierce I saw one maul a woman, but what could I do? This dog just sat there panting, with his tongue hanging out.

I stretched out my hand. He sniffed it. Then licked it. He seemed nice. Maybe I wouldn't die by dog bite today.

I took in the sight of a bone-weary horse tied to a low-sided wooden hay wagon that looked like it was about to fall apart. "Up, Max," said the farmer, and the dog jumped into the back.

"It's a short trip," said the farmer. "You can ride in the back with Max, or you can walk beside the wagon." He patted his shirt pocket. "I'll keep your papers safe so you won't escape into the woods."

"If you're not Herr Huber," I asked, "where are you taking me?"

"To *Frau* Huber, my daughter," said the man.

So, there was a farmer named Huber. I felt a little bit better about that.

I almost decided to walk so that I could avoid the dog, but I was so exhausted and hungry that I took a chance. I settled in the hay as far from Max as I could, being careful not to upend the tippy cart. The horse clip-clopped down the road, and I shivered in the autumn breeze. Many worries weighed me down, but it did feel good to be outside in the fresh air and sunlight instead of a stuffy boxcar or a dank storage room.

The dog stretched out in the hay and rested his head on my shin. I wasn't sure if that was to stop me from jumping off, or whether it was a friendly gesture. He looked up at me with liquid brown eyes that seemed intelligent—and kind.

I was thirsty and felt grubby, but for the first time since Salzburg, I also felt a bit of hope. The thought of working for a female farmer was encouraging. Maybe Frau Huber was a good person. Nathan wanted me to be safe, and maybe I would be safe at the Huber farm. I also knew where Nathan was. Maybe I would be able to visit him, or at least send him a letter.

All around us were snowcapped mountains that seemed vaster than our own Carpathian range. Were these the Alps? This area was far away from the fighting, and these mountains might protect me from bullets and bombs. If Germans sent their own children here to be safe, maybe it would be safe for me as well.

We were on a narrow dirt road that ran along a river and when I sat up tall and looked across it, I could see what I assumed was Innsbruck itself. Through the trees, I got glimpses of tall pastel buildings, churches, and monuments—none of them looked like they had been damaged by bombs.

If only Nathan were with me, I would have been happy with this choice, fleeing into the heart of Hitler's birth country. It seemed that the farther I traveled from home, the more peaceful it was.

We passed green rolling hills and lots of trees. The houses were smaller now, and in some ways reminded me of home. These brown-roofed houses were whitewashed with lime just like those in Viteretz. Out of one of the houses came a woman in a skirt and embroidered apron. She unfurled a colorful patchwork quilt and shook it vigorously to get the dust out. The sight made me ache with longing, and my mind filled with the image of Mama, standing at our own door as she'd air out our down comforters. What was Mama doing now? Did she miss me as much as I missed her? And what of Krystia? Would she now think that I was as brave as her?

Or would she think I was just *foolish*?

But then an image of Nathan formed in my mind. Maybe he wasn't with me, but bridge building in Salzburg was safer than the ghetto in Viteretz. He was out of the war zone. Away from the units that hunted down Jews.

Not foolish.

Never foolish.

As long as the people I loved were safe.

After a few kilometers, the wagon turned off the road and entered a lane that I hadn't noticed because of all the trees. As we rounded the corner, I caught my breath at the sight of a wide vista with one large house, barns and sheds, and vast vegetable fields. Was all this land for just one family?

The house was even larger than the Commandant's in Viteretz, although it wasn't as fancy-looking. There was a long wooden table under a tree in front of the house and the shed beside it was the size of our house. Beside the shed was a chicken coop surrounded by a grassy yard. A dozen or more chickens ran in and out of the coop and all over the grass, pecking at the ground for seeds. Beyond the house was an open hilly meadow dotted with trees and rocks and a few large buildings.

There were cows. I counted them: eight!

Back home, we had dear Krasa, our one cow; she slept in the narrow shed attached to our two-room house. Krystia would loop a rope around Krasa's neck and take her on the two-kilometer trip to our pasture twice a day. Everyone who had a cow in Viteretz did the same. These Austrian cows were not tethered, nor were they fenced. They roamed free on the low hilly pasture with tall mountains behind them, munching grass to their heart's content.

Frau Huber must be wealthy to have such a huge house and so many cows and chickens.

As the wagon pulled up the lane, I looked out at the field on my left side. It was filled with long rows of beets, carrots, winter cabbage, and onions. Yet for such a lot of vegetables, and with frost in the air, why were there just half a dozen workers?

On the right side were fields of potatoes. A pink-scarfed woman guided a horse and plow through one of the furrows, but the plow was made for someone taller and the horse wasn't very cooperative. A woman with a straw hat knelt half a row behind her, picking potatoes by hand, and another six bareheaded women were a few rows over, working as a group.

The old man pulled his wagon up in front of the shed by the house. "You get out here," he said.

Max jumped down ahead of me, running to the cows in the pasture.

"See that building?" he said, pointing beyond the storage shed and chicken coop. "You'll find your living quarters in there. Freshen up, then come to the house."

"Sir," I said, "could I have my papers back?"

The farmer shook his head. "I'll keep them safe for you."

I gave a slight bow, thanked the man, and tried to hide how angry I was. He wasn't trying to help: He just didn't trust me.

I walked to the building in the meadow and stepped inside. It reminded me of Auntie Polina's barn on her farm in the country, but this one was larger, with two rows of cow stalls facing each other on the main floor, and a hayloft above.

I was supposed to live in a cow barn? I stepped inside to get a better look.

The stalls were clean, and some were strewn with fresh straw, and those seemed to be used for cows, not people. But as I walked down the aisle, I saw that some were not in use but three in the middle were being used by people. In one, there was bedding neatly folded on a bed frame made of tree branches, and various items of clothing hung from nails. On the back wall was a handmade crucifix and off to the corner hung a bent and faded photograph of a serious-looking young man with thick eyebrows and an angular nose. The stall directly across from it had a willow bed with a worn pillow, but the stall didn't look as if it were being used. The one beside it had a few handmade beds in a stack, plus a couple of pillows and folded blankets. Obviously not all the field workers were sleeping in here.

At the far end of the barn was a table made from an old wooden door, with tree stumps for legs. There were dented milk cans instead of stools, and stacked on the table was a mismatched assortment of cups, bowls, and cutlery. A straw broom was propped up against the far wall and a washbasin and pitcher sat on a stand by the door, with worn towels and washcloths hanging from nails.

Around the back was an outhouse and water pump. I splashed water over my face and hands, then swallowed down huge mouthfuls of cold fresh water. Feeling cleaner, more awake, and no longer thirsty, I headed back to the house to await my fate.

CHAPTER SIX
FRAU HUBER

The pink-scarfed woman stood in front of the house, hands on hips and an annoyed look on her face. She was just a few inches taller than me, thin but wiry. She wore a baggy pair of men's overalls and heavy work boots. Her cheeks were freckled and chapped from too much sun.

This was Frau Huber? She looked so young.

I stood up straight.

"You're *it*?" she asked.

"There were two of us," I said. "But Nath . . . Bohdan was taken off at Salzburg."

She threw her hands up in frustration and turned toward the house. "*Vater*," she called. "You were supposed to bring me eight foreigners."

The old man opened the door and stepped onto the porch. "I'm not a magician, Beatrice. There was only this young girl."

"How does the army expect me to fulfill our produce quota if they keep hauling my workers off for other things?" she asked.

"Don't yell at me for it," he said. "I'm just as frustrated as you are."

She turned back to me and said, "And you're just a child."

I bristled with anger. Seeing how few workers she had, I hardly thought she should be criticizing me. At least she wasn't likely to send me away.

I pasted on a smile and bowed slightly. "Frau Huber, I'm almost twelve and I am an experienced farmworker."

"I hope so," she said. "But I could use a dozen of you."

She pointed to the straw-hatted young woman in the potato field who was working on her own. "You can help Bianka, but first go get some more burlap sacks from the shed beside the house."

A chicken collided with my ankle as I walked past a frenzied cluster of them to step inside the shed. At the end of one shelf was a stack of burlap sacks. I grabbed as many as I could carry.

As I walked past the group of workers to get to my spot in the field, I noticed that not only were their heads all bare, but each had very short hair. One of them looked up at me as I passed, and she bobbed her head in greeting, so I nodded back to her.

I set the bags in the furrow across from the solitary woman and knelt beside her. As I brushed off potatoes and put them into a sack, Bianka looked up and smiled. She seemed to be about my age.

I worked in silence, glancing at her from the corner of my eye from time to time. Once Bianka's last sack was filled, I handed her one of mine.

"*Danke,*" she said.

"*Ich heisse* Maria," I said, holding out my hand in greeting. My name is Maria.

"Where are you from, Maria?" she asked in Polish.

"Viteretz," I responded. "Not far from Lviv."

"You say Lviv, not Lwów, so you must be Ukrainian."

"I am," I said. "And you're Polish?" To me, Polish sounded like Ukrainian spoken with a lilt, and while not all the words were the same, it wasn't difficult to have a conversation with someone who was speaking Polish.

She nodded. "From Warzawa."

Warsaw had been under Nazi occupation for longer than we had. I knew that from listening to Mama and Uncle Ivan.

"Were you taken, or did you sign up?" I asked her.

Bianka sighed. "I was captured two years ago when I was twelve."

She was fourteen, nearly three years older than me. "I volunteered this week," I said.

Her eyebrows raised in surprise. "You *volunteered*?"

"It's a long story," I said.

We worked in silence for the rest of the morning, leaving the bags in the field as we progressed. As I tied the neck of the last burlap bag, I sat back on my heels and looked around. The group of six workers had bagged a row and a half of potatoes, and Frau Huber had plowed up two new rows, but we were still bagging our first row. There were dozens of rows. She really did need more workers. Frau Huber untethered the horse, and as she led it out of the field, she paused in front of us, her brow wrinkled in a frown.

"I allow you to take up to two potatoes from the field each day, but don't let people see you do it."

Frau Huber had vegetables, potatoes, milk, chickens, and eggs, yet we were supposed to sneak potatoes out of the field? It didn't make sense. When she was out of earshot, I asked Bianka, "What was that all about?"

"I'll explain later," said Bianka, arching her back and wiping sweat off her brow.

Frau went inside her house. A minute or two later, she stepped back out, holding a pot and lid, which she loudly banged together.

Bianka slipped a couple of potatoes into her skirt pocket, then stiffly pulled herself off her knees, grimacing all the way. As she stood, I noticed that she had the letter P sewn onto the front of her dress. "It would be helpful if you could also take your two potatoes," she said.

It seemed like stealing, even though Frau Huber told us to do it. I bent down and picked up two potatoes. Maybe I would understand after being here for a while.

I must have straightened up too quickly, because suddenly the world spun. Bianka grabbed onto my arm to keep me from falling.

"Are you okay?" she asked.

I gulped in some air. "I'm just dizzy."

"When was the last time you ate?" asked Bianka.

When was it? Nathan and I had shared our bread and cheese on the train with the others, but was that a day ago, or more? And it was just a bite. "I'm not sure."

She held my elbow. "You'll feel better once you're out of the sun. And you need something in your stomach."

I leaned on Bianka until we were out of the field and into the laneway. The half-dozen women who had also been picking vegetables walked in front of us, while the short-haired workers bagging potatoes were a few steps behind us.

The door of the farmhouse opened, and an older woman stepped out. "Lunch is ready," she said to the workers in front of us.

The delectable scent of roasted chicken with onion and fresh baked bread wafted from the open door. My mouth watered at the smell of the good food and my stomach began to ache. How long had it been since I had eaten? The six women ahead of us walked up the steps and into the kitchen, but Bianka stayed frozen at the foot of the steps.

"We shouldn't make them wait," I said to Bianka, putting my foot on the bottom step.

"That food is not for us," she whispered.

"But the other workers are all in there . . ." I was so hungry.

Bianka dug her fingers into my elbow.

The older woman noticed us through the glass. Moments later, she opened the door, holding a basket of black buns that were each the size of my palm. She gave one to each of us.

"Go now," she said.

"But what about . . . ?" I began to say.

"Thank you, Frau Lang," Bianka said as she pushed me toward the barn. Once we were out of earshot, she said, "That's Frau Huber's mother. The man who brought you here is Frau Huber's father."

When we stepped inside the barn, the cool shade was a welcome relief. Bianka set her bun on a plate and I did the same. The other workers came in and each took a spot around the table, ceremoniously setting their buns on plates as well.

Bianka opened the lid to one of the dented milk cans and placed her two potatoes inside. "Put yours in there as well and sit down before you fall down," she said.

I did as she said and sat down gratefully, but noticed that none of the other workers took anything out of their pockets. "Why did we take these potatoes?" I whispered to her.

"Don't worry about that right now," she said.

Bianka filled a pitcher with water and set it in the middle of the table. A girl who looked to be the oldest of us all set out eight metal cups. Bianka filled one of the cups and handed it to me right away.

"Drink," she said urgently, sitting down beside me.

I felt seven pairs of eyes watch as I drank the cold water. As I set my empty cup down, I noticed, again, everyone's very short hair.

I looked at the girl who had set out the cups and said, "My name is Maria. What's yours?"

"Hania," she said, taking a big bite of her bread and chewing.

"Eat, Maria," said Bianka. "We'll talk later." She pulled off a big chunk from her own bun and shoved it into her mouth, chewing it so quickly that she couldn't possibly be enjoying it.

I bit into my bun and slowly chewed, trying to figure out what it was made of. There were husks of wheat and maybe barley and peas in it. The texture was so solid that I needed sips of water just to get it down. Even so, I savored the fact that I was filling my stomach. It wasn't chicken, but at least it was food. And I was so very hungry.

All eight around the table silently chewed. When I was about halfway done with my bun, a woman's silhouctte appeared at the entrance.

"Where are the rest of the foreigners?" said a clipped voice in German.

As she strode toward us I could see her round cheeks. Her blond hair was pulled back into a low bun. She looked to be a bit older than Mama, because where Mama's face was smooth, this woman had finely etched wrinkles around her eyes. She wore a brown jacket with a white armband and a skirt.

The workers stood up, so I scrambled to my feet as well. "Good afternoon, Frau," I said in German. "I am the only newcomer."

"I am not a Frau," she replied in German. "I am Blockleiter Doris Schutt."

I bowed slightly. "I'm sorry, Blockleiter Schutt. My name is Maria Fediuk."

She slapped me so hard across the face that I nearly lost my balance. "Where is your badge?" she asked.

"I . . . I just got here," I said, gripping the table. "I've not been given a badge to wear."

She slapped me hard again. "You're not given the badges; you pay for them, you pig."

She reached into her pocket and pulled out a stack of badges, some labeled with OST and some with P. "Where are you from?"

"Viteretz, near Lviv," I said.

She counted out five badges with P on them and threw them onto the table. "Pin one on now, and sew the rest onto your other items of clothing. Do not be caught without a P or you'll be getting more than a slap the next time."

Bianka scrambled from her chair and came back with a safety pin. With shaking hands, I pinned on one of the badges.

We all stayed standing as the Blockleiter strutted through the barn, nudging the straw with the tip of her shoe here and there, tugging at the clothing hanging in Bianka's stall. She didn't check the milk tins and didn't find our hidden potatoes.

As she was about to leave, she turned to me and said, "Frau Huber will dock your pay for the cost of those badges."

When the Blockleiter was finally out of earshot, Bianka slumped back onto her stool. "She is such a horrible woman. How were you supposed to get badges when you only just arrived? But at least the inspection is over with for the day."

"Who is she?" I asked.

"The Blockleiter. Every neighborhood around here has one. She reports to the Nazi government for the area. She doesn't just keep track of the foreign workers. She also reports back on the Hubers and Langs and other Aryans."

Bianka's explanation surprised me. Austrians were considered equal to Germans. I could understand why the Nazis wouldn't trust us foreign workers—we hated them—but why did they need to watch the locals? Once I was here longer, maybe it would make sense.

My cheek still stung from the Blockleiter's slap. I had to keep out of her way.

"She comes every day at the same time?" I asked.

One of the other girls shook her head. "I've seen her here at all different times. When she's on a rampage, she confiscates things—usually our food—which is why we eat it quickly."

"Once she even took my blanket," said Bianka.

I looked down the table and saw that all the girls were chewing slowly now and enjoying every bite that was left of their buns.

"Why is this all we get for lunch?" I asked, turning what was left of my dry black bun around in my hand. My stomach was still yearning for oniony chicken and fresh white bread. "Why aren't we eating with the rest of the workers?"

"Didn't you notice that all of us here are wearing badges?" said the girl across from me.

I looked around the table and realized that they all wore OST badges. Bianka and I were the only ones with a P.

"What's the difference between the badges?" I asked.

"The P means Poland and OST stands for *Ostarbeiter*, or Eastern worker from Soviet Ukraine," said Hania.

"Why didn't I get an OST?" I asked. "I'm Ukrainian."

"The part of Ukraine you're from was Polish before the war, so you wear a P like me," said Bianka.

I was about to protest but one of the girls said, "We're all Ukrainian. I'm Uliana from Kyiv. Count yourself lucky. The OST badges are the worst. With the P you'll get slightly better treatment."

The girl sitting to the left of Uliana stood up and reached out her hand. "My name is Valentina, and I'm from Kharkiv." She nodded toward the girl on her other side. "That's Lisa from Vinnytsia."

Uliana pointed to the two girls beside her who looked like they could be sisters and said, "This is Oleksandra and Daria. We're from Rivne."

"Why don't the workers at the house wear badges?" I asked.

"They're Aryan workers," said Bianka. "We're Slavs. They get to eat the same as Germans, but our ration is six hundred calories a day."

"Those women are Aryans?" I asked. "But they're working in the field just like us."

"They're guest workers from countries allied with the Nazis," said the girl across from me. "They could be Dutch, Danish, or maybe Norwegian."

In a crazy way, this all did make sense. It was similar to what the Nazis were doing back home, treating everyone differently depending on their race: Jews were killed, Slavs were enslaved and starved, Aryans did the plundering and killing. Here in the Reich, though, it seemed like there were even *more* categories, because Slavs could be P or OST and some Aryans were from other countries.

We all finished our buns, and while I listened to the others as they chatted, I looked around the barn. There were eight of us, but it didn't look like there were eight places to sleep. I guess I would find out where everyone slept later on.

Just then, Frau Huber banged her pot and the six girls wearing the OST badges got up from the table and rinsed out their cups.

I stood too, but Bianka put her hand on my arm. "That's only for the OST girls. We still have another fifteen minutes," she said. "Frau Huber will bang her pot again when it's time for us to go back to the field."

I sat back down, and the other girls left.

"Grab the potatoes and follow me," said Bianka.

She set a ladder to the loft and climbed up, with me close behind. I followed her to the far back corner, where she pushed aside a bale of hay and got down onto her knees. She pressed her palms flat on one of the floorboards, then rocked it back and forth until it came out. She lifted out the one beside it too. Inside the hiding space was a burlap bag. She opened it wide. I knelt beside her and looked in. More potatoes, but also other vegetables and even some apples. We added today's haul.

"Why do you . . . ?" I began, but Bianka held a finger to her lips. I stayed quiet until we got back down the ladder.

"Why do we have to hide food?" I whispered.

"That's our insurance," said Bianka. "For the times the

Blockleiter or some other official goes on a rampage about Slavs eating too much."

It all seemed so hopeless. Why had I thought that coming here would be a solution to my problems? "I should never have signed up to work in the Reich," I said.

"Not true," said Bianka. "We're lucky to be in this area. Frau Huber is as kind as she can get away with, and even though we're not fed much, we won't starve."

Bianka's words made me feel a little bit better, but I felt selfish being safer and better fed than Mama and Krystia. And my noble reason for escaping—to help Nathan—had now become complicated. If I could send money home, I would feel better about my choice. And if I could somehow still help Nathan, then I'd be happy with my choice. But could I do those things? I had no idea.

Just then, Frau Huber banged her pot and we walked back to the field.

CHAPTER SEVEN
GUSTAVE

Frau Huber didn't return to the fields in the afternoon; instead Uliana used the plow. She was a bit taller than Frau Huber, so she was able to work it quite well. The Aryans didn't come back to work when Frau Huber banged her pot for us, but about half an hour later when I stood and stretched, I saw that they were back in the fields again. Aryan workers obviously got a longer midday break than P or OST workers.

"Frau Huber must be very rich with all this land," I said to Bianka as I continued to pick potatoes, brush them off, and put them into bags.

"Her harvest belongs to the Reich as long as the war is on," said Bianka, sitting back on her heels and stretching her arms out wide. "If she doesn't meet her quota, the Nazis could take the farm away."

Bianka's words shocked me. Frau Huber could be punished for feeding us more than six hundred calories a day, and she could lose her farm for not making enough food for the Nazis. She was Aryan, and she wasn't a slave, but in some ways she was also trapped, just like me and Bianka.

I looked at the vast field of potatoes around me, and I felt like weeping. All this food was going to feed Nazi soldiers, yet people back home were starving. Each time I put a potato into a burlap sack, was I helping Hitler kill the people I loved? The thought made me want to vomit.

Bianka must have realized what I was thinking, because she put her hand on top of mine and gave it a little squeeze. "Each potato *we* eat is one less that goes to soldiers," she said.

I had already taken my two potatoes for the day, but I picked up another, and brushed off the dirt with my skirt. I looked around to make sure no one was looking, then bit into it, savoring its juicy freshness. Bianka picked one up too. She gave me a big smile as she took a bite and chewed.

It seemed overwhelming, fighting Hitler one potato at a time, but Mama always told me to fight back in small ways that were in my power. Even Bianka and me surviving was a way of fighting back. I looked up into the cloudless sky and whispered under my breath, "I *will* survive, I *will* help Nathan. I *will* help Mama and Krystia. And this is one potato the Nazis won't be eating."

Toward the end of the afternoon, the eight of us OST and P girls helped Herr Lang load his wagon with the sacks of potatoes. As he guided the horse off the field, and we walked a few meters behind him, I picked up a potato and put it in my pocket. Bianka gave me a dirty look.

"Get rid of it," she whispered.

"But you said . . ."

"Dump it," she hissed.

I knelt, pretending to adjust my shoe. I dumped the potato onto the dirt.

A military truck appeared through the trees and braked at the end of our field. A soldier stepped out just as Herr Lang and his wagon got there.

"Load it up," said the soldier, opening the gate on the back of the truck.

We took turns hefting the bags of potatoes into the back of the truck, and when we were finished, the soldier said, "Line up, all of you."

The eight of us stood in a row and the soldier patted each girl's clothing, looking for hidden potatoes or vegetables. "You're clean. You can go."

Now I understood. If I had been caught stealing a potato, I would have been punished. I was so thankful for Bianka's guidance. I could have been in trouble so many times already if she hadn't been willing to help me. And what about Nathan? Was anyone helping him stay out of trouble as he worked on the Salzburg Bridge? I hoped and prayed that he had met someone kind and helpful like Bianka.

When we got back to the house, the door opened, and the scent of sausage and garlic wafted out, making my stomach grumble. Frau Huber stepped out, a bundle of something tucked under her arm. "OST girls," she said. "Come to the barn with me."

Uliana, Valentina, and the others followed her, chattering with excitement. Bianka and I walked a few steps behind. I was filled with curiosity. What exciting thing was happening to them and not to us?

Once we were all inside the privacy of the barn, Frau Huber said, "It's uncooked rice today." She patted each girl on the shoulder as she gave out the soft cloth packets. "Hide them well."

As Frau Huber exited the barn, I watched as the OST girls helped one another open the packets and hide the grain a teaspoon at a time in seams and folds all over their clothing.

"Why are you hiding rice in your clothing?" I asked Uliana.

"The guards will be here shortly to take us back," she said, tucking her blouse in and smoothing the waistband of her skirt to ensure the rice didn't show.

"They live at the local slave camp," said Bianka. "You and I are the only ones who stay in the barn."

"Oh," I said. "And the guards do a search just like the soldier did?"

"Yes," said Uliana.

"What do they feed you at the camp?" I asked.

"All we get at the camp is watery soup and bread made of wood chips," said Uliana. "Working at this farm is a luxury. If Frau Huber didn't help us, we would starve, and so would our bunkmates."

"Line up," I said. "Let's pretend we're your guards."

Bianka and I methodically patted down every seam and fold in each of the OST girls' blouses and skirts, smoothing down the rice to a single layer in each hidden place that we detected so that even the most thorough guard wouldn't find it.

We had just finished when Max's barking announced another vehicle had arrived.

"See you tomorrow," I called out as the OST girls trudged out of the barn.

After they left, I walked toward the pump, intending to get some water, but when I passed our table, I noticed that someone had set a covered dish on it. I took the lid off: fried sausages and cooked vegetables, still warm.

"That's from Frau Lang," said Bianka. "She brings us good food when she can."

I sat down heavily at the table and held my head in my hands, overwhelmed with gratitude, but also with guilt. This was more food than what Krystia and Mama would be eating back home, even with only two mouths to feed. And what about Nathan? Was he fed watery soup and wood-chip bread? How could he keep up his strength on that? "We are very lucky to be working for kind people," I said.

Bianka got out two bowls and divided up the stew. "Eat up quickly," she said. "The Blockleiter isn't the only one spying on us here, and we're eating Aryan food."

I followed Bianka's lead, eating the stew as fast as I could, even though I longed to linger over it. When it was all gone, I licked my bowl.

Bianka got up from the table, gesturing toward the dirty dishes. "Can you clean those very carefully and put them back like they were?" she asked. "If anyone comes in here, they can't know that we've had stew."

"What about this covered dish?" I asked.

"Leave it on the table once you've cleaned it. Frau Lang will pick it up."

I cleaned the dishes in cold soapy water while Bianka went to her stall. By the time I was finished with the dishes, she had come back. "Time to help Frau Huber with the cows," she said. "Come outside with me."

All eight cows were slowly ambling their way toward the barn. I couldn't imagine Krasa knowing how to get to our shed or our pasture without being led, so how did these cows know to come to the barn? I shaded my eyes and looked toward the pasture. There was Max, trotting in circles around the back hooves of the last cow, nudging her with his nose toward the barn along a well-worn path.

Once inside, each cow stepped into a stall without prompting. Frau Huber followed behind them with a bag of feed, so I hurried over to help her, scooping out a small quantity of feed and putting it in the trough in front of each cow to relax them for the milking. This was the same thing we did for Krasa back home.

Once they were all contentedly munching, Frau Huber handed me a pail and pointed to the cow in the stall at the far end. "You start with Brunhilde and work your way to the front of the barn."

At home, it was usually Krystia who milked the cow, and as I leaned my face against Brunhilde's udders and sang a lullaby to make her milk come down, I felt terribly homesick.

Bianka worked her way down the cows on the opposite side of the aisle and we got into a rhythm with both the milking and our lullabies. Even though my fingers ached, this simple chore reminded me of Krystia. It was like a little bit of home.

Frau Huber stood on the back of the hay wagon and we passed each pail up as it was filled so she could pour the milk into a metal drum. By the time all the cows were milked, there were three drums on the back of the wagon plus part of another drum that she set aside, likely for her own household.

A military truck pulled up outside the barn and took the three drums of milk away.

As the cows settled down for the night, Bianka changed out of her work clothes and into a floral dress and a knitted wool sweater.

She handed me a blanket and said, "Hang your work clothing outside and let's go up to the loft to find you something to wear for bed."

I slipped off my dirty clothing and washed with cold water at the pump, then wrapped myself in the blanket and followed her up the ladder.

Bianka pushed two bales of hay aside to reveal a

wooden crate. She knelt in front of it and lifted the lid, revealing a tidy stack of folded cloth items. "I'm a bit of a collector," she said as she rooted around. "Anything Frau Huber throws out, I keep. Anything another worker leaves behind, I keep. Here's something," she said, passing me a long-sleeved flannel nightgown that buttoned up the front.

I slipped it over my head. "It fits perfectly."

"I think it used to belong to Frau Huber's daughter," said Bianka.

"I didn't know she had a daughter," I said.

"She has a son and husband too," said Bianka. "They're both in the army. The daughter is busy with school and her club, but you'll meet her soon enough." Bianka continued to look through the box. She pulled out a child's white blouse and a dark skirt. "These would fit you," she said, "but they're not something you'd want to wear." She folded them carefully and put them back in the box and continued to look through the layers. Her eyes lit up. "Here's what I was looking for," she said, handing me a sweater.

It was soft brown wool and looked very cozy. I pulled it over my head. Like the nightgown, it fit me perfectly. I felt clean and warm. "This is wonderful," I said. "Thank you."

"The cows give off a lot of body heat, warming up the barn, but I still get chilly at night," said Bianka. She kept sorting through the box, then drew out a blanket and handed it to me.

It was light gray wool and soft, but it was worn all the way through in a couple of places. Someone had added colorful patches here and there with meticulous stitching. Whoever had owned it had practically loved it to death.

"Thank you, Bianka," I said. "Where did you get this?"

"The Hubers threw it in the trash," said Bianka, sitting back on her heels. "And Gustave took it," she said with a sigh.

"Gustave?"

"He was a French soldier," said Bianka. "A prisoner of war. He was sent here as a forced laborer two years ago, around the same time I came."

"Where is he now?" I asked.

"Taken to do heavier work, or to an armaments factory, I would imagine," said Bianka. "That's what happens to all the men."

I held the extra blanket up to my face. It felt soft and comfortable and smelled of soap flakes. "Why didn't he take this when he left?"

"They took him right from the field," said Bianka. "He couldn't pack. He couldn't even say good-bye."

As she looked at me, I could see tears welling in her eyes. Did he and Bianka have a special bond just like me and Nathan? It seemed that Bianka and I had more in common than I realized.

"Are you sure it's okay for me to have this blanket?" I asked. "It looks like you put it up here for safekeeping."

"I thought that he might come back," said Bianka. "But I never heard from him again."

"How long ago was it that he left?"

"Four months, and not a single word from him," she said.

"Just four months? He could come back," I said. "I should leave this up here."

"Four months is a lifetime during a war," said Bianka. "And if Gustave is still alive, if we meet again, he'll be happy to know that a nice girl like you got to use his blanket."

Her words made me smile.

As I carried my blanket through the barn, some of the cows seemed to watch me, while others ignored me. Most were lying in their fresh straw, although Brunhilde was standing. She nudged me with her nose as I passed, and I scratched her head affectionately, thinking of my own dear Krasa.

My bed was comfortable with the two blankets and the pillow, and even though there was a chill in the air now that it was getting darker outside, I was warm in my heavy sweater and nightgown. I looked over at Bianka and saw that she was sitting in her bed, holding the photograph that had hung on her wall.

"Is that a picture of Gustave?" I asked.

She looked up at me with tear-filled eyes. "It is," she said. "He gave it to me about a week before he was taken away."

I lay down in my bed and closed my eyes to give Bianka some privacy with her memories and worries.

As I tried to get to sleep, I imagined looking through the photographs that Mama had back home. In my mind I saw her and Tato on their wedding day. They both looked so hopeful, young, and in love. Nathan's father had taken that photo and he'd even been able to capture the sparkle in Mama's eye. Mrs. Segal was also a photographer, and she'd taken a picture of me and Krystia and Mama together on the first day the Nazis had come to our town. We were so joyful, thinking that the war was about to end. Little did we know back then that the Nazis were worse than the Soviets. Mama's one photograph that hadn't been taken by Nathan's parents was of Auntie Stefa, Mama's older sister who lived in Toronto, Canada. Auntie looked so much like Mama, except her cheeks were fuller and she had nicer clothing. I loved looking at that photograph because it showed me what Mama would have looked like if we hadn't been plunged into a war. She'd sent us many packages of items from Canada that she thought we could sell. After Tato had died, the money Mama made from selling things from those packages had kept us from starving. Auntie Stefa had pleaded with Mama to come live with her in Canada. She said it would be better for us there. But then the war started . . .

How I wished I had a picture of Nathan. What was he doing right now? Had he found a friend? Were the workers who built Salzburg Bridge given enough to eat? Or did they have a way to sneak in more food? Did he have a blanket and pillow to sleep on? Had they discovered that he was Jewish? A shiver ran up my spine. If they found out, they would execute him. Should we have stayed hiding in the woods instead of signing up for work in the Reich? It was impossible to know, but we had made the best decision that we could at the time. I thought of Mama's words, about changing what could be changed and not fretting about what couldn't. Easier said than done!

I heard Bianka settle down into her own bed and her breathing became rhythmic with sleep before the sun had fully set. I was sure that our day would start early tomorrow, so I tried to do the same, but all I could think of was Nathan and Krystia and Mama—the three people I loved most in all the world and the three people that I might never see again.

CHAPTER EIGHT
DEBORA

It's not easy falling asleep to the smell of eight cows belching and farting. Or the sound of eight cows shifting around and groaning. There were other noises in that barn as well—wood creaking, a small something slithering, and the sound of mice (or were they rats?) cracking seeds with their teeth. But cows radiate heat and my blankets and sweater were cozy, so I hardly noticed the draft that seeped through the gaps in the wood. I was thankful for Bianka's friendship, and was grateful to be on a farm with kind owners, away from the fighting, with food to eat and a place to sleep.

I dream that Krystia stands at my bedside. "Why did you leave me and Mama?" she says, her arms folded.

Nathan appears next in my dream. "A bite of sausage is all I ask," he says. "And maybe some help with building this bridge?"

Nathan's face transforms into Mama's. She puts her hands on my cradle and rocks me like a baby. My heart aches with regret.

"Maria, you need to get up."

I opened my eyes. In the darkness, I could make out the silhouette of Bianka shaking my willow bed, not Mama rocking my cradle. That's when I heard the rooster and sat up with a jolt. "It's morning already?"

"We've got to get on with the chores," said Bianka.

My eyes were still blurry with sleep as I changed into my work clothes and began milking the first cow. We filled the milk drums one pail at a time, and when we were finished, I was wide awake, with a sore back, aching hands, and a growling stomach. There was a quarter of a pail of milk left over after three and a half drums were filled, so Bianka and I split it between us and we drank it down. I savored the warm, creamy taste and relished the feeling of a stomach that was temporarily full.

I was about to sit at the table but Bianka said, "No time for a break yet. We need to clean the barn."

I helped Bianka fetch the shovels and a wheelbarrow and started on the disgusting job of cleaning out the manure from eight dirty cow stalls.

"For the last while it's been me alone doing this job," said Bianka as we finished the last one. "I'm grateful for your help."

We scrubbed our hands and faces with cold water and soap. It felt good to be finished with that awful job and to be somewhat clean again. My skirt and blouse smelled bad, but there was nothing to change into and no point anyway—we were about to be called to the potato field.

Bianka went up to the loft and threw down a couple of bales of straw into the center of the barn. While she was up there, she got a potato from our hiding place.

"What if the Blockleiter catches us eating that potato?" I asked as she cut it into two pieces and handed me one.

"Just don't let her see it," said Bianka.

I slipped the half potato into my pocket and we spread the fresh straw out with rakes, making sure that the floor of each stall was covered. It wasn't until this chore was done that we rested for a few moments over a cup of water and our half a raw potato each.

On my third bite Frau Huber banged on her pot. I popped the rest of the potato into my mouth and scurried out the barn door behind Bianka as I chewed.

The next twenty-four hours were a repeat of the first, only Frau Lang couldn't sneak us extra food because the Blockleiter spent much of the afternoon and early evening at the farm, going over the account books and inventory.

A couple more days passed, and as we sat down at the table after our usual chores one evening, I realized that I had lost track of the days. "When is the next Sunday?" I asked Bianka.

"In two days," she said.

"Can we walk into town and find a church?"

Bianka gave me a strange look. "Sundays aren't much different than other days."

"But the posters," I said. "We're supposed to get Sundays off."

"The posters," said Bianka, rolling her eyes. "You know those posters lie."

"We don't get time off on Sunday?" I knew the posters lied about some things, but surely there was a little bit of truth in them?

"Even if we did get Sunday off, we couldn't go to church," said Bianka. "Forced laborers aren't allowed in churches. They're not allowed in stores or theaters or restaurants."

"But I need to send a letter to my friend in Salzburg and I need to send one to Mama as well."

"We're not allowed to send letters back home either," said Bianka.

"But how will I send money to Mama, then?"

Bianka gave me a pitying look. "Even if you could send a letter, where would you get this money to send back home?"

"They don't pay us?" I asked.

"You'll get a paper that says you're paid," said Bianka. "Frau Huber does pay the Nazis for our labor and the money is supposed to be held for us in a bank, but for foreign workers they tax almost all of it back. I've never actually been given money."

I cradled my head in my arms, feeling utterly defeated. There were two reasons I had signed up for work in the Reich. One was to help Nathan escape, and the other was so I could send money back home to help Mama and Krystia survive the Nazis' Hunger Plan. Nathan and I were separated, and I had no idea how he was doing, and now I knew that I couldn't even get money to Mama and Krystia. I was such a failure—and a tired and hungry failure at that.

"Cheer up," said Bianka, and I felt the warmth of her hand making circular motions on my back. "Even being on a bad farm is better than being at a work camp, and this is a good farm. And we're far away from the war zone."

I took a deep breath and lifted my head. "That makes me feel like a coward," I said. "I thought I could do something, help the people I love, somehow make it better for them, but I've only managed to run away and leave them all in danger."

"How have you left your friend in danger?" asked Bianka.

Her question brought me up short. Could I trust her with my secret? Would she report me to the Blockleiter for helping a Jew? I couldn't be sure.

"My friend had to escape," I said, deciding to be as vague as I could. "He needed my help, but we were separated when the soldiers took him off at Salzburg."

"Your friend was Jewish," said Bianka. It wasn't a question, but a statement.

Should I tell her? I couldn't meet her eyes. I just stared straight ahead.

Bianka whispered, "I wish I had been able to help Debora."

"What happened?" I asked.

"Debora was a friend from school," she said, reaching out and clasping my hand. "She and her family were forced out of their home at gunpoint. The Nazis blocked off three square kilometers of Warsaw and rounded up all the Jews—about four hundred thousand—of our city. They were crammed together. No space, almost no food. And then the Nazis began to build a wall—to brick them all inside."

I squeezed her hand.

"Before the wall was completed, Debora somehow managed to escape. She came to our house."

"What did you do?"

"I was frightened," said Bianka. "If we were caught hiding her, Mama and I could have been shot. I was alone when she came to our door. Instead of being brave and letting her inside, I told her I needed to ask Mama first."

Bianka's voice faltered. Her eyes filled with tears. "I asked her to come back in an hour. When Mama came home, she was furious with me. She said that if it were the other way around, Debora would have hidden me right away."

Bianka laid her head down on her arms and wept.

"Did Debora come back?"

Bianka lifted her tearstained face. "No. She was caught. A policeman shot her right in our street. If I had hidden her when she asked, Debora might still be alive."

What could I possibly say to comfort her? Similar horrible events had unfolded in my town as well. The Nazis ruled by terror and we all lived in fear.

"It was my hesitation that killed Debora," said Bianka. "A neighbor saw her at our door and reported us to the Gestapo. As punishment, Mama and I were both shipped off to the Reich as slave laborers. If I had taken Debora in right away, maybe none of this would have happened."

Bianka's story brought back images of my Jewish friends and neighbors and how they had been imprisoned and then shot.

I looked in Bianka's eyes and saw the pain.

"Do you know where your mother is?" I asked.

Bianka shook her head. "I don't even know if she's still alive."

"What about your father?" I asked.

"I don't know about him either. He was an officer in the Polish army. The last I heard was that the Soviets arrested his unit in 1939."

We sat there, side by side in silence, for a while, then Bianka said, "You didn't finish telling me about your friend."

I told her about Nathan's escape from execution, and his papers identifying him as Bohdan Sawchuk, and how we had planned on hiding in plain sight, working in the Reich as foreign laborers.

"If you had been on the run for months together, I'm sure he can pass himself off as Ukrainian by now," said Bianka. "You did help him."

"But he's in Salzburg and I'm here," I said. "It makes me so worried."

"He'll blend into the crowd of foreign workers."

CHAPTER NINE
HITLER GIRLS

The Blockleiter began dropping in unexpectedly more than once a day. Had someone told her that the foreign workers were being fed more than was legal? I could only hope and pray that it wasn't the case and that soon Blockleiter Doris Schutt would find something else to be interested in.

A couple of weeks passed with very little in the way of extra food. While I was getting mightily sick of hard black bread, raw potatoes, and the occasional mouthful of milk, I was more worried about the OST girls. They could sneak bites of potato and vegetable while they worked in the fields, but they couldn't risk trying to smuggle such bulky items back into the camp for their friends. I worried that their friends might starve.

And then as October turned to November, the OST girls stopped coming to the farm altogether. When I asked what happened to them, Frau Lang said their entire camp was assigned to work in a munitions factory. I was a bundle of nerves, thinking of our friends doing such dangerous work. And it made me sick to think of them helping our enemy make more weapons. I also wondered whether the story was really true or they were actually taken from the farm because someone found out they were being given extra food. The Aryan guest workers still lived at the farm, eating and sleeping in the house and working their shortened hours, but without the OST girls, the bulk of the hard work fell to me and Bianka.

One night, Herr Lang surprised us with a visit after the cows were bedded down. He held onto a bulge under his shirt: two thick slices of rye bread slathered with lard. "Doris just left. She's very interested in this farm," he said as he gave us each a piece of bread. "She's practically been living in our kitchen, going through the ledger with Beatrice and threatening to send someone else in to manage the farm."

"Would she actually do that?" I asked, taking a big bite of the bread and chewing it slowly. The bread was fresh, and the lard was filling. It was so kind of Herr Lang to risk sneaking it to us.

"She would if there was someone else to run it," he answered. "But anyone more qualified than my daughter is fighting in the war."

"If she had more workers, there wouldn't be a problem," said Bianka, pulling off bits of her bread and popping them into her mouth. "I wish our OST friends could work here instead of at the munitions plant."

"If only I could create more workers out of thin air," said Herr Lang. "Good night, girls, and thank you for your hard work."

As I enjoyed the rest of my rye bread, I thought about the possibility of Frau Huber losing her farm. She and her parents were kind and they were caught in Hitler's web almost as much as me. But the shortage of farmworkers was probably happening all over the Reich. If Nazi soldiers couldn't get enough to eat, maybe the war would end. Maybe Nathan wouldn't be hunted for being Jewish anymore and we would both be able to go home.

That thought thrilled me.

Bianka and I had just finished cleaning out the manure and were sitting at our table with half a potato each and a cup of water, waiting for Frau Huber to bang her pot, when the silhouette of a girl filled our doorway. I quickly shoved the potato into my pocket, hoping that the intruder wouldn't see it.

When she walked toward us I saw that she had blond

pigtails, and while she seemed young, she was taller and heavier than either of us. She was dressed in an old skirt and blouse and heavy shoes, so at first I thought she was a new foreign worker.

"That's Sophie, Frau Huber's daughter," whispered Bianka.

I knew Frau Huber had a daughter, but she had slipped my mind. I had been here nearly a month and had never seen her before. Bianka stumbled to her feet as the girl walked up to our table.

"Good afternoon, Fraulein Huber," said Bianka.

"What's her name?" Sophie asked, jerking her head toward me.

"I'm Maria Fediuk," I said, getting to my feet.

Sophie pointed to the bulges in our pockets. "Does Frau Huber know that you've stolen from the fields?"

"Fraulein, we must eat something," said Bianka, her face white. "Otherwise we'll faint and get no work done."

"Our produce quota is nearly impossible to meet. I can't imagine Frau Huber letting you Slavs eat whatever you want."

Anger bristled through me at her words. Why didn't Bianka tell Sophie that Frau Huber told us to take potatoes? I thought about saying this but reconsidered. Maybe Sophie snooped for the Nazis just like the Blockleiter.

Bianka held out her last bite of potato, her head cast down. "Fraulein, would you like to take this?"

Sophie crossed her arms. "Now you're being insolent. If the Blockleiter catches you stealing produce, we could all be in trouble."

"I'm sorry," said Bianka.

"You need to be on your best behavior today." Sophie's face lit up with a smile. "I've managed to convince my unit leader to let the League of German Girls help with the harvest. Several units are joining in. Finish up here and report to Frau Huber. The girls should be arriving within the hour."

With that, she turned and left.

I held my breath as she walked away, and when she was out of earshot, I asked Bianka, "Why does she call her own mother Frau Huber instead of *Mutter*?"

"Hitler's rules. Those in the League of German Girls are his children, not their parents' anymore."

"They don't wear uniforms here?" I asked.

"Usually, she does," said Bianka. "But that was old clothing she had on. Probably so she doesn't ruin her uniform with field work."

I thought about the dark skirt and white blouse that Bianka had kept in her clothing stash. Sophie was tall and strong. I couldn't imagine her ever being small enough to fit into that tiny skirt and blouse. "How old was she when she started in that Hitler club?" I asked.

"Aryan girls are required to join the junior group by the time they're ten years old," said Bianka. "She turned fourteen this year and is now a full-fledged 'Hitler Girl.'"

"So she's been calling her own mother Frau Huber for the last four years?"

Bianka nodded. "I can't imagine how horrible that would be, witnessing your daughter's mind being warped against you."

My heart ached for Frau Huber and that made me think of my own mother. Even though I was far away from her, Mama knew that I loved her and that Krystia loved her too.

There were Hitler Girls in Viteretz too, and I knew one of their members—Marga. She would march around in uniform with her group and sing songs that praised Hitler. She was brainwashed into hating Poles and Ukrainians and Jews and she tormented my sister. I bit into the last of my potato and slowly chewed. "It should be an interesting day, working side by side with girls who hate us."

The front door opened just as we got to the house, and Frau Huber stepped out. Instead of wearing her usual overalls, she wore a dirndl—a traditional German woman's peasant skirt, blouse, and apron. Her hair was braided and coiled around her head and her face was flushed pink. I'm sure it was from embarrassment because she looked ridiculous.

My own shock at her appearance must have shown on my face, because she said, "This is my daughter's doing. She reported me to her unit leader. Apparently, my work clothing does not live up to the Nazi feminine ideal."

So her daughter *was* a snoop.

We stood beside her and watched as a truck pulled up in front of the fields. The back was filled with girls who laughed and chattered among themselves. None were wearing their official uniforms but were instead dressed like Sophie, in worn skirts and blouses appropriate for field work. They hopped off and walked over to Sophie, who stood at the edge of the potato field beside a wheelbarrow stacked with burlap sacks. She handed each girl a couple of sacks and pointed to what part of the field that girl should go to. The first truck pulled away, another one arrived, and more girls piled out. In all, there were four trucks and about sixty girls, who acted more like they were going to a party than working in the field.

From the passenger seat of the last truck, an athletic-looking woman got out and strode toward us. She was dressed much like the Blockleiter, only her suit was more tailored. She didn't look to be that much older than the girls she supervised. "*Heil* Hitler," she said, saluting. "I take it you're Sophie's mother, Beatrice Huber?"

Frau Huber saluted back. "I am," she said. "And you are Gruppenführerin Winter?"

"Yes," said the group leader. "What a beautiful dirndl you're wearing." She stepped back a bit to take in the full glory of Frau Huber's costume. "You are a credit to Aryan womanhood."

Frau Huber opened her mouth, but no words came out. Her hands clenched but she meekly nodded.

The group leader turned her attention to us. "These Slavs cannot work in the field today," she said. "My girls shouldn't be in such close contact with subhumans."

"Yes, Gruppenführerin Winter," replied Frau Huber. "I was going to have them help me prepare a lunch for the girls."

"Sophie told me you have Aryan guest workers living here. Why not get them to help you?"

"My parents have taken the guest workers into town today," said Frau Huber. "So that leaves just me, and these two Slavs."

The group leader clicked her tongue. "Not good planning."

Her eyes landed on Bianka's filthy clothing, and then on mine. I could feel my face going hot with shame.

"See that they're bathed and dressed in clean clothing before they come in contact with food served to my girls," she said.

"That was the plan, Gruppenführerin Winter," said Frau Huber.

"Off with you, then," said the group leader, with a dismissive flick of her wrist. She turned and walked a few steps toward the potato field, then stopped and looked back. "I've requested extra rations to be delivered so you can make the girls something special for their dessert. It should be arriving any time."

With that, she strode off.

When the group leader was out of earshot, Frau Huber muttered, "This is going to be a long day."

"Frau Huber," said Bianka. "Do you want us to go back to the barn and wash up? We could put on our sleep outfits. They're cleaner than our work clothes."

Frau Huber frowned in thought. "There should be some old dresses here that you can use. Come with me to the washhouse. I had been warming up water for the laundry, but I guess that will now be your bathwater."

Bianka bathed first since she had been at the farm longer, and I helped her wash her hair, vigorously scrubbing her scalp with the bar of soap. When it was my turn, the water was gray and scummy, but I didn't mind. It felt so good to plunge into warm water instead of trying to clean myself with an icy sponge bath at the pump. Bianka lathered my hair into a froth and then I closed my eyes and dunked under, rinsing off all the soap. Even though the water was brown, I felt so clean and refreshed as I stepped out of the tub.

Frau Huber had brought fresh slips and underwear as well as soft worn cotton housedresses. We both dried off and slipped into the clean clothing, then tiptoed barefoot across the grass to the back door of the house.

"Put these on," said Frau Huber, handing us each a pair of socks.

As she ushered us through the hallway, we passed an opened door. I caught a glimpse of a long room with a row of bunk beds on either side. Six of the beds looked like they were in use. So this was where the Aryan guest workers slept.

Frau Huber saw me glancing in. "If it were up to me, you two girls would be sleeping in there instead of the barn, but the Blockleiter has forbidden it."

We passed an indoor bathroom, with a white enamel sink, a flush toilet, and even a tub. Beside the bathroom was a set of stairs going up to the second floor. Across the hallway from the bathroom was a cozy sitting room with bookshelves. Above the fireplace were two pictures. One was the usual photograph of Hitler, and beside it was a photograph of Frau Huber and family. The fact that she was the only one not in uniform made me shiver. Sophie smiled proudly in the white shirt and black scarf of the League of German Girls, her brother was a regular soldier, and Herr Huber was an officer of some sort.

At the front of the house was a dining room with a table for eight and a glass-fronted china cabinet, displaying tarnished silver service ware and dusty crystal and china.

Across from that was a large kitchen, and it seemed to be the heart of the house, with a long wooden table, a six-burner woodstove, icebox, and a sink with taps instead of a pump. I imagined a scene before the war with all of Frau Huber's family and farmhands gathered around the table eating together, with everyone equal and no one in uniform.

As we stood waiting to be told what to do, a couple of soldiers came into the kitchen and deposited packages on the kitchen table: a cotton sack of sugar and another of flour, both from Ukraine, and a tin of lard and raspberry preserves from Poland.

All last winter, the Nazis went from house to house in Viteretz, confiscating practically all the food they could find. How many people had starved so these Hitler Girls could have their treats?

Frau Huber assembled measuring cups, bowls, and bakeware on the counter, and she hummed a tune under her breath. "We'll make rosti from our own supplies for their lunch, and with what we got from the warehouse, we'll make Linzer cookies for dessert."

As Frau Huber measured out ingredients for the cookies, Bianka and I peeled a whole lot of potatoes for the rosti. Linzer cookies were basically a nutty shortbread dough rolled out and cut into circles that were baked and then assembled like little sandwiches with jam in the middle. During every step of the process, my stomach growled, reminding me that all I had eaten since yesterday was half a raw potato. How I would have loved to eat a spoonful of the cookie dough or a dollop of jam. It was downright painful, assembling those sweet treats on an empty stomach.

We made enough cookies so that each girl would be able to have at least three of them if they wanted. Once the cookies were cooled and assembled, Frau Huber arranged them in artful pyramids on a couple of large metal trays. There were some left over so Frau Huber put them away for when her parents and the guest workers came back from town.

She reserved two cookies and gave one to each of us. I put the whole thing into my mouth and chewed slowly, reveling in the burst of raspberry and nutty sweetness. Eating that one cookie made me even hungrier, though, so when the time came to fry up the rosti, it was agonizing to be enveloped in the scent of sizzling bacon, onions, and fried potatos.

Frau Huber transferred each fresh batch of rosti into giant roasting pans that she'd kept warm in the oven. Once all the rosti were finished, we cracked dozens of eggs and fried them up, then garnished the rosti with the eggs.

Frau Huber banged a pot and lid together on the porch to let the Hitler Girls know it was time to come out of the fields for lunch. As the girls washed their hands at the water pump, Bianka and I used oven mitts to carry out the steaming pans of rosti and set them on the long table outside. We hefted stacks of plates and cutlery, pitchers of fresh milk and glasses. The girls lined up and served themselves, talking and joking. Some sat at the table, but most relaxed cross-legged in groups of twos and threes on the grass and chattered happily as they ate.

Bianka and I ran around, making sure to replace dirty dishes with clean and to wipe up any spills. The Gruppenführerin stood to one side, a plate of rosti balanced in one hand. She observed her girls' behavior and also ours as she carefully chewed small forkfuls of rosti.

As we carried a near-empty rosti pan back to the kitchen, Frau Huber touched my shoulder and whispered, "Eat this leftover rosti, but don't let anyone see you." In a louder voice, she said, "Please bring out the dessert."

Bianka and I each brought out a tray of Linzer cookies and I watched the Gruppenführerin's expression slowly turn to a smile as we set each pyramid of cookies down for her girls.

Most of the girls lined up in an orderly way for dessert, but one abandoned her half-eaten plate of rosti under a tree and ran to the cookies.

The action filled me with rage. These girls were given so much while others starved and they didn't even appreciate it.

All at once, there was a loud clap. "Unacceptable," shouted the Gruppenführerin.

The chattering girls stood rigid, suddenly silent.

"Rita, do not take a cookie until you have finished your lunch."

I stifled a smile as the girl backed away from the cookies but was surprised by the fear on her face. She walked back to her abandoned plate and slumped down to eat in solemn silence.

Was every single person, even those most favored, being watched and judged and risking punishment?

And what sort of punishment did a Hitler Girl get if she disobeyed?

Bianka and I slipped back into the kitchen, away from the chatter. As the door closed behind us, I was relieved to be away from those privileged people.

We heaped two plates with delectable leftover potato and egg and I stood at the edge of the window so I could see out to the Gruppenführerin, but she couldn't see me. The rosti was delicious and filling and I enjoyed every mouthful.

Washing the pots and pans and dishes after serving sixty girls was a big task and it took a couple of hours, but it was a nice change to be working with soap and water instead of digging up potatoes or shoveling manure.

Frau Huber came inside midafternoon. "The girls have harvested the potatoes and are now working on the vegetable fields."

"Does this mean you'll meet your quota?" asked Bianka.

Frau Huber nodded. "The army will get what they want. I just hope they'll leave enough potatoes and vegetables to get us through the winter."

"Those supplies should help over winter," I said, pointing to the flour and sugar and preserves that the soldiers had dropped off.

"That doesn't stay here," said Frau Huber. "When you've finished the dishes, can you please pack it up? When the truck comes for the produce, they'll also be taking this back."

"The League members are treated very well," I said.

Frau Huber nodded. "They get treats, special trips, attend Nazi rallies. I barely see Sophie, and when I do, we argue. It's like she thinks the Nazi Party is her true family."

"Yet without Sophie's intervention, the harvest would have rotted in the fields," said Bianka. "She did that to help *you*—her real family."

Frau Huber took a deep breath. "You're right, she did. But it scares me, the things she thinks and does."

CHAPTER TEN
SOMEONE ELSE'S DRESS

Sophie's intervention with the harvest meant that the Blockleiter allowed Frau Huber to keep her farm, and that was also good for me and Bianka. We were so very fortunate to be living with a kind family in the safety of the Alps. And while I felt glad for my safety, what good did it do when the people I loved were all still in danger? I'd had no way of communicating with Nathan since we'd been separated and no way to contact Mama and Krystia either. I could only hope that we'd all survive and be reunited after the war.

With the field work finished, the Aryan guest workers left. Bianka and I settled into a less frenzied routine, mostly looking after the cows and chickens.

Sophie spent so much time with the League of German Girls that it was almost as if she didn't live on the farm. She had a bedroom in the house, but she spent many nights away. Even when she was at home, she'd leave early and wouldn't get home until past dark. The only time I ever saw her was on the odd Saturday when she wasn't called out for a rally or a project. That meant that the only person who was always watching was the Blockleiter. She would drop by at odd hours trying to catch us off guard. What was her reward for catching a forced worker eating an extra piece of bread? Did she get paid in money or food? Or did she just enjoy tormenting us?

It was essential that we be busy whenever the Blockleiter came by, so in addition to looking after the livestock, Bianka mostly assisted Frau Lang in the washhouse with the laundry. She also helped Herr Lang sort out and store seeds and repair worn farm equipment.

Herr Lang slaughtered an old cow that no longer gave milk and he exchanged half of it with a neighbor for a pig carcass. Bianka and I both helped Frau Huber cut the meat into portions and hang the cuts in the cold cellar.

The mending became one of my chores and Frau Huber would give me mounds of cow blankets, canvas sacks, and work clothing to patch and repair. I also spent a lot of my time going between the kitchen and the cold storage in the root cellar as I helped Frau Huber store away the portion of the harvest she had been allowed to keep. I liked it best when we worked together in the kitchen, processing the harvest bounty. Her method of dehydrating herbs, berries, fruits, and mushrooms was just like Mama's, only on a larger scale. She had traded some of her potatoes and vegetables with a neighboring farmer for apples and peaches, and so we made jams and jellies as well.

Frau Huber had a radio in the kitchen and what we heard most was German announcers talking about the latest German war successes. I knew that they tried to make everything sound positive from a German point of view, and for me that was terrifying. My stomach would lurch every time the announcer talked about the latest exploits in what he called the Eastern Front—what I knew as home. Frau Huber's reaction was the opposite of mine because the Huber men were fighting on the Eastern Front. Her husband, Karl, was an officer in the Sixth Army and her son, Otto, was a machine gunner.

When she heard those same successes that terrified me, she'd give a prayer of thanks.

But when the announcers' stories were about the Allies' air operations in Northern Italy, we were both upset. "If they can bomb Northern Italy, they'll soon be able to reach us," said Frau Huber. "We're just the other side of the mountain."

Much as I wanted the Allies to win, I didn't consider Frau Huber and her parents to be my enemies. I didn't want a bomb to land on them, or on me, Bianka, or Nathan either!

But despite the scary news, Frau Huber and her parents thought the war would end soon.

"Our boys will be home any time now," said Herr Lang as he came back from town one day with an armload of groceries. "The war has to be ending—look at all this food!"

When I unpacked what he'd been able to buy, I shook my head in wonder. Real coffee, more sugar, flour, and *chocolate*. With this in addition to the eggs, milk, butter, and cream from the farm, it was if there was no wartime rationing at all, at least not for Aryans.

One day in mid-December, the Blockleiter invited herself into the farmhouse, so Frau Huber asked if she'd like coffee. It was good timing because we had just made cookies that morning. While the two women sat at one end of the long kitchen table and chatted, I set down a pot of freshly brewed coffee, a bowl of sugar, and a pitcher of cream. The Blockleiter glanced briefly at me, then frowned. She said to Frau Huber, "Just think, once we win the war and everyone comes home, you'll be able to get rid of these Slav subhumans and get your Aryan farmworkers back."

I could feel my face go bright red. Didn't that woman realize that I had a life and family of my own that I'd dearly like to get back to? And the reason that I was here was because of the war that her precious Hitler started?

I went to the counter and picked up a plate of Linzer

cookies, and as I set them on the table in front of the Blockleiter, Frau Huber said, "My girls may be Slavs, but they're hard workers. I could just use more of them."

And much as I appreciated Frau Huber's comments, they made me angry as well. In some ways she was just one step away from Blockleiter Doris Schutt in her attitude toward me and Bianka. Not once had she asked about my family, or Bianka's, or what life we'd go back to when the war was over. She didn't really see us as her equals, only as workers.

Doris picked up one of the cookies and nibbled on the edge. "My favorite cookies," she said. "And these are especially tasty."

"Maria made those," said Frau Huber.

The Blockleiter looked down at her cookie, then up at me. Her eyebrows rose in surprise. She looked back at Frau Huber and said, "You did a good job of teaching her."

I felt like picking up the plate of cookies and dumping them on her head. Cookies were not difficult to make if you could afford the ingredients. Each Christmas before the war, Mama, Krystia, and I would make *medivnichky*—honey cookies—together. They were much tastier than Linzer cookies, in my opinion, and took more skill to get just the right texture. I looked at Doris and pasted on a pleasant smile.

I took my anger out on the counter by scrubbing it vigorously as Frau Huber and the Blockleiter continued to chat.

"Have you heard anything from Headquarters about the war on the Eastern Front?" Frau Huber asked.

"Your husband, Karl, is in the Sixth Army, isn't he?" Doris asked.

Frau Huber nodded.

"He'll be in Stalingrad, then," she said. "We'll push out the Soviets any day now." She took a sip of coffee. "What division is Otto in?"

"The Twenty-First Panzergrenadier Regiment."

"Both of the Huber men are in Stalingrad," said Doris. "You have two war heroes in the family who will soon be on their way home."

"The fighting at Stalingrad has been going on for a long time," said Frau Huber. "It makes me so worried."

"Don't you worry about your boys," said Doris. She held up her cup. "This is real coffee, not chicory. Our side must be winning."

Not long after that, Frau Huber came home from the post office with a big package and a grin on her face.

"Pass me those scissors," she said, setting the box on the kitchen table.

I got up from my mending and brought the scissors over to her. "Do you know who the package is from?" I asked.

"From Karl, on the Eastern Front," she said.

The Eastern Front was my home, and I was terrified

to think of what must be happening to the people who lived there. Frau Huber hadn't heard anything from her husband in a long time and I tried to feel happy for her that she'd finally gotten some news. While I knew what it was like to be separated from the people I loved, I couldn't feel much sympathy for her. All I could feel was fear and anger. Each time she heard something good from her husband or son, it would be bad for my family and friends.

She snipped the string on the outside of the box and cut through the packing tape as well. Most of the box was filled with straw, but at the bottom was something wrapped in white tissue. There was a note card tucked in the folds of the paper.

She opened the envelope and read the card aloud:

Beatrice, my love—the war will end soon—that I promise.

Can you imagine a future Sophie, dressed like a princess, with you and me both by her side? Cherish that image as I do. Our family will be whole again soon. Your loving Karl.

Frau Huber tore open the tissue to reveal a wedding dress of handmade lace.

"How exquisite," she said, shaking it out and holding it up by the shoulder seams. "It's the kind of dress I always dreamed of my daughter wearing on her wedding day."

I ran my fingers over the bodice, admiring the edging

of seed pearls. The Sophie I knew suited a uniform more than a wedding dress.

As I admired the fine lacework, I noticed a tiny thread that had caught in the fabric by one of the cuffs. "Would you like me to fix that?" I asked, pointing it out to Frau Huber.

She looked at the catch and frowned. "Yes, please do. Give it a light steaming too, then hang it in my wardrobe."

I cleaned off the kitchen table and spread the dress out, carefully examining it for any other damage. There were no more catches.

But there was also a burst pattern of tiny dark dots near the bottom of the skirt.

"What a disappointment," said Frau Huber, squinting her eyes to see them. "Do you think you can get it out?"

She stood beside me as I dabbed one of the dots with a damp cloth, but instead of disappearing, it bloomed out into a red smudge. "This is blood," I said, feeling sick.

Frau Huber's face went pale. "Sophie will not wear this dress," she said. "Clean it. A friend sells dresses in the city. She'll get rid of it for me."

I was able to remove the blood, but I wept as I worked.

That night I dream of a bride at gunpoint in the woods. She removes her dress and sets it to one side. The bullets jolt her off her feet and she falls into the waiting grave. A mist of her blood lands on the dress.

CHAPTER ELEVEN
FOR GOOD LUCK

My birthday was on December 14, but it passed without me even noticing. It wasn't until a few days later that I realized I was now twelve. If I had been at home, Mama and Krystia would have tried to make something special to eat, even if we had practically nothing. And they'd sing *Mnohaya Lita*—"Many Years"—to me. Instead I sang it under my breath as I wiped down the kitchen table. And I wondered how many years it would be until I saw Mama and Krystia again.

I was startled out of my thoughts by a knock at the door. "Are you Beatrice Huber?" asked the soldier standing on the doorstep. He struggled to keep hold of a large box in his arms.

I'd had enough of boxes and their surprises, but it wasn't up to me to refuse it. I guided him inside and he set it on the kitchen table. "I'll get Frau Huber for you," I said.

I hurried to the washhouse, where I had last seen Frau Huber, and told her that she had a military visitor. She followed me back, white-faced with fear.

"Good news," said the soldier, thrusting an envelope into her hands. "Your son is coming home on furlough. He'll be arriving by train in Innsbruck on Thursday afternoon, just in time for *Rauhnacht*." He gestured toward the box sitting on the kitchen table. "That's a Führer's Package," he said. "Extra rations of meat, fat, sugar, and flour so you can prepare special foods for his return."

"This is wonderful," said Frau Huber. She took a deep breath, then walked the soldier to the door. As he turned to leave, she asked, "Do you have any news about my husband, Karl? He's an officer in the Sixth Army."

The soldier hesitated for a moment before speaking. "I'm sorry, but I have no news, and the holiday furlough lists are final. If you haven't heard, his furlough won't be in time for the holidays."

Frau Huber looked troubled as she closed the door behind the soldier, and I didn't blame her. That package from her husband with the bloodied wedding dress seemed almost like a curse.

Sophie got time off from both school and the League of German Girls for the holidays. I was at the sink scouring a pot when she shrugged off her winter coat to reveal her uniform: a crisp white blouse with a swastika patch sewn on the left sleeve. She wore a black tie that was fastened around her neck with a brown leather knot. Her skirt was black and it came just below her knees. She set a paper bag on the kitchen table and grinned. "Look at what Gruppenführerin Winter gave me to decorate our tree with."

I dried my hands and walked over to peer inside. There were all sorts of small shiny items, but it was hard to see exactly what they were. At home we decorated our tree mostly with cookies, nuts, and apples, but Tato had made a small good-luck spider web out of silvery wire before he died and that ornament always had the place of honor. During the first part of the war, when the Soviets had occupied Viteretz, we weren't allowed to celebrate Christmas, so we didn't have a tree at all. And then when the Nazis invaded, they took our food. We did have a small tree, but no cookies, nuts, or apples, so we put Tato's spider web ornament on it, and hoped for good luck.

Sophie reached in and pulled out a silver swastika the size of her palm. It hung from a hook and it had a silver bell attached to the bottom. I had a sick feeling in the pit of my stomach just looking at it.

"What does that have to do with Christmas?" I asked.

"*Christ*mas?" she said. "We celebrate *Rauhnacht*. Christ was a Jew. Why would we celebrate a Jew's birth?

Our celebration is to give tribute to our holy father, Adolf Hitler."

Rauhnacht—rough night? Her blasphemous words took my breath away. She must have mistaken my stillness for interest.

"We have a box of our own *Rauhnacht* ornaments in the cold cellar. We've been collecting them for years, but it's always nice to get new ones." She reached into the bag and pulled out something large that was wrapped in tissue paper. "The Gruppenführerin even gave me a new star for the top of our tree." She removed the tissue to reveal a large red swastika.

I held onto the edge of the table, trying my best not to react to the horrible items she was showing me. She dug through the box and pulled out another ornament. "This one's kind of interesting." She opened her palm.

"What is it?" I asked.

She held it to the light so I could get a better look. "A hanged Jew swinging on a scaffold," she said, grinning. "Isn't that funny?"

"No, it's not funny," I said. "It's celebrating murder and it's sick."

Her eyes widened with surprise. "Are you criticizing me? Take that back."

I stood there, staring her down. I would not take it back. If her own mother wouldn't tell her these things, someone had to.

She punched me hard in the stomach. I bent over double, not able to breathe. Two hands pushed my head. I fell to the floor. Sophie's knees dug into my back and she gripped my wrists in her hands.

"Get off me!" I screamed.

The weight of her knees left my back and I struggled to turn around, but it was hard to do because she was still holding onto my wrists. Sophie pulled me up to my feet, and as I struggled to keep my balance, she pushed me toward the root cellar. "Is this what they teach you at your club?" I asked. "How to hurt and to hate?"

"You talked back to an Aryan," she hissed. "I should kill you, but my mother needs your labor, so count this as your lucky day."

She forced me down into the root cellar, then slammed the door behind me, bolting it shut.

I stood there, dazed at what had just happened. Did I really criticize Sophie to her face? Bianka would be horrified, but my heart and gut told me that I had done the right thing. I couldn't just stand there and listen to her hateful talk without reacting. But as I leaned against the dirt wall and tried to catch my breath, my head told me how foolish I had been. Any Aryan could shoot me, and it wouldn't be considered a crime.

I was locked in this root cellar. Even if I got out, I was locked into this life. I curled into a ball on the floor and wept.

What kind of world did I live in where people like Sophie thought it was funny to hang a replica of a murdered Jew onto a Christmas tree?

An image of Nathan hanging from a noose filled my mind. Was that his fate if he stayed in the Reich? How could I stop that from happening? I felt so powerless.

I stayed huddled on the cold dirt floor, rocking back and forth and weeping. Somehow, I must have slept.

A warm hand rested on my shoulder. I opened my eyes, but the root cellar was dim. I bolted up to a sitting position.

"You're fine, child. It's only me."

Frau Lang was holding a warm mug to my lips.

"Sip," she said. "Chicken broth."

I took a sip of the salty liquid and let its warmth envelop me. Mama used to make chicken broth before the war. She would always make it if I had been sick. Tears sprang into my eyes, and I let out a huge uncontrollable sob.

"Sophie told me what happened," said Frau Lang.

How could I respond to a comment like that? Was Frau Lang about to reprimand me for talking back to her granddaughter? Would she justify the hateful ornaments for their tree? She held the mug to my lips again and I took another sip of broth. The fluid felt good on my throat, and it also gave me strength.

"I'm not going to apologize," I said.

"My dear girl," she said. "I can't tell you how many times I've wanted to argue with Sophie myself. There's a madness in her, with all this Hitler brainwashing."

I took a sip of broth and swallowed it down. "So, you don't think the way that she does?"

"That should be obvious," replied Frau Lang.

"You've been kind to me and Bianka," I said. "And I know you could be punished for that."

"I'd give you more if I could get away with it," said Frau Lang. "My husband and daughter feel the same as me. But Sophie could have all of us sent away, not just you and Bianka."

"She'd do that to her own family?" I asked.

"She used to be such a nice girl," said Frau Lang. "We need to tread carefully while she's at home for the holidays. And you need to apologize."

CHAPTER TWELVE
SPASIBO

One of the hardest things I ever did was grovel to Sophie.

"I accept your apology," she said with a smug smile. "And now that you've learned your lesson, I'm sure you'll behave."

Herr Lang cut down a fir tree and put it in the corner of the dining room. Sophie decorated it herself, with the terrible new ornaments that had come in the package from the Gruppenführerin. The tree didn't look very festive to me and seemed to give the exact opposite message of the peace and love that a Christmas tree should convey. One thing I was grateful for was that she didn't put the hanging Jew on the tree. "In case you're wondering why," she said to me as I dusted the dining room table, "*Mutter*, I mean, Frau Huber won't let me put it up. She says it would clutter the tree and take away from its overall beauty."

Knowing Frau Huber, I was sure she saw no beauty in

that Nazi tree, and I was grateful that she'd found a way to keep the most horrible decoration off it.

Sophie did insist on supervising me and Bianka as we baked and cooked all sorts of goodies. I think she wanted to make sure we didn't eat any of them, and it truly was torture to cook these delicacies while eating just two small black buns a day.

That didn't stop Sophie from taking samples of everything we made. "It will be such a treat to have Otto home. I want all the food to be to his liking," she said, smacking her lips as she licked a spoonful of batter.

We made tarts, tortes, candies, and puddings. And she produced another surprise gift from Gruppenführerin Winter: a cookie cutter in the shape of a swastika. "This way, the Linzer cookies are truly a fitting tribute to Hitler."

I had seen many Reich soldiers over the past year, in Viteretz, while on the run, and during our train ride here, and I knew that the true Nazi believers were those with the letters SS on their collar. The best that I could hope for from one of those was that they'd look through me, not at me, because then I would be safer.

I did not relish the prospect of Otto living, eating, and sleeping in the farmhouse. To be in the same household as a Reich soldier was a terrifying thought. But when he arrived on Christmas Eve, he surprised me. For one thing, the corners of his collar were adorned with nothing more than two bars. No SS, no Death's Head skull, or swastika either, just those bars and an eagle over one pocket.

He favored his left leg and he leaned on a crutch to get around, but when Frau Huber asked him where he was injured, he'd laugh and say, "Stalingrad."

His cheekbones stuck out on a too-thin face and his skin looked like tanned leather. And at dinner that first night when I was about to set down a heaping plate in front of him, I nearly dropped it in shock. He looked straight into my eyes and said in Russian, *"Spasibo."*

"You're welcome," I answered in German.

"Aren't you from Russia?" he asked with an easy smile. "I picked up a bit of the language on the Eastern Front."

"I'm Ukrainian," I said.

"Ah, the granary of Russia," he replied. "Our tanks went all the way through, from Lvov to the steppes. Communes and wheat, as far as the eye could see."

His words made me squirm. I blurted out, "It's Lviv, not Lvov. Russian and Ukrainian are different cultures, like Austrian and German. You're all part of the Reich now because of Hitler, and we were part of the Soviet Union because of Stalin, but that doesn't mean I like it."

"Maria, shut up," said Sophie, reaching over to her brother's plate and popping a curl of his fried onion into her mouth. "It's not a subhuman's place to be lecturing an Aryan."

Otto flashed his sister a look. "If you could see how these *subhumans* are fighting us in the East, you might have a bit more respect for their intelligence and bravery," he said.

Sophie's eyes widened at his comment, but she didn't respond.

Frau Huber sat across the table from Otto and she had been silently watching the exchange between her children as she absentmindedly stabbed a bit of rösti with her fork. "Son," she said, now that there was a lull in conversation. "Have you heard anything from your father? When I was last in Innsbruck, there were rumors that the Sixth Army has been encircled by the Soviets in Stalingrad."

Otto looked down at his plate and didn't respond right away. Then he looked up at his mother and said, "*Vater* is still in Stalingrad, but we'll get them out. I promise you that."

I stayed silent for the rest of the evening, clearing plates as need be and putting out the sweets and coffee at the end of the meal. I was extremely grateful when dinner was over, and I was finally released.

•   •   •

"I have a surprise for you, Maria!" said Bianka.

She grabbed my hand and led me past the cows to our table at the other end of the barn. It was set with three tin cups and three plates, and there was a covered dish off to one side.

"Are we having someone join us?" I asked.

Bianka smiled. "Have you forgotten that this is Christmas Eve?"

Ukrainian Christmas Eve was not until January 6, but this was Polish Christmas Eve. In Polish and Ukrainian traditions, an extra plate was always set out on Christmas Eve to welcome the wandering stranger. Bianka reached underneath the table and brought out a tin can filled with dirt. She set it in the middle of the table.

Bianka reached under the table again. This time she brought out two fir branches. She handed one to me. I held it to my nose and breathed in deeply, a sob catching in my throat as the resinous scent reminded me of home. "Did you cut these down?" I asked. "I hope we're not going to get into trouble for that."

"Herr Lang brought them, but I waited for you to get here so we could put our tree up together." She stuck her fir branch into the tin can.

I took the one I was holding and inserted it beside Bianka's.

"That's not all."

From her pocket, Bianka drew out a delicate silver star on a hook. Not a swastika, but a five-pointed star with a cross in the middle. "Herr Lang said that this has been in his family for generations, but they haven't used it since Hitler came into power." She reached up and hooked it onto one of the boughs.

I patted the extra plate. "For the wandering stranger, and dearly departed," I said.

Bianka nodded. "And for our friends who can't be here." She got up from the table and went to her sleeping stall. A moment later she came back with the photograph of Gustave. She propped it up beside the empty plate.

How I wished I had a photograph of Nathan. And of Mama and Krystia too. I closed my eyes and imagined them together, smiling at me.

"Herr Lang brought us wiener schnitzel and rosti," said Bianka, uncovering a dish. "But we'll save that for tomorrow."

Christmas Eve was a time for fasting—no meat for Ukrainians or Poles—so we had our usual black buns instead. We sat down together, Bianka and me, nibbling our buns, surrounded by the low groans of sleeping cows and under the bough of our fir branches. I was thankful for the deep friendship that had developed between Bianka and me. And I was grateful for the decency of the

Langs, Frau Huber, and Otto. As I chewed small bites of bun, I thought of Mama and Krystia. I prayed that they had enough to eat and that they weren't angry with me for leaving them. I thought of Nathan too, hoping that he had food and warmth and friendship too.

Otto stayed until after New Year's Day in 1943, and a stream of relatives and neighbors dropped by, mostly to see if Otto had any news about their own sons. From the bits I was able to overhear, it sounded like every young man from the Ostmark was fighting at Stalingrad.

While he was at home, Otto reinforced the wood on our barn. He and I stood side by side in the crisp January air. "Thank you for fixing the barn," I said.

"You've been such a good help to my family," he said. "I don't know how they would have managed without you."

Much as I realized that he meant to be appreciative, his comment made me cringe. I had mixed feelings about assisting anyone who was working on the Nazi side. I had come here for my own goals—to help Nathan escape and to earn money so Mama and Krystia could survive the war. This farm was producing food for my enemy, and while I was helping the wrong side, what had I done for Mama, Krystia, or Nathan?

Nothing.

Here I had done all this work, yet I had no money to send home. And what about Nathan? I had no idea what was happening with him and I certainly wasn't helping him.

There were many things that I wanted to say to Otto, but I controlled myself. I pasted on a smile and said, "You're welcome."

Otto pointed west toward the Alps. "If I were on the run," he said, "that's the way that I would go, following the railway line."

His comment took me by surprise. Had he read the conflicted emotions on my face? Was this enemy soldier giving me advice about running away?

"You mean through the mountains?" I asked, keeping my voice calm. "What's on the other side?"

"Liechtenstein. Switzerland. Neutral countries."

My gut told me that Otto was trustworthy. "Your family has been good to me," I said. "And for that, I am very grateful."

I tossed and turned that night, thinking about Otto's comment about neutral countries. I was safe for the moment at the farm, and if I did have to escape, I'd go back home, to Mama and Krystia, not farther away from them.

But what about Nathan? His mother had already been executed by the Nazis. His father was part of the Underground, which made false documents to help Jews escape. Hopefully, he'd be able to get out himself as well and he would probably try to get to a neutral country. There would be no one left for Nathan to go home to in Viteretz.

I was sick with worry that he would be found out and killed before the war ended, or he would be worked to death building the Salzburg Bridge. What if he could get to one of those neutral countries? As I drifted off to sleep, a plan began to form in my mind. I had to see Nathan face-to-face, to tell him of the rail lines that went from here to neutral countries.

Most of that next day, Otto worked with Herr Lang in the warehouse, trying to repair broken-down farm equipment. He tinkered quite a bit with a motorized tractor but couldn't get it to work.

"Such a shame," he said over dinner. "All the tractor factories are making war weapons. Our tractor could be up and running if I could just get my hands on a few replacement parts."

"Good thing the army left us our two old horses," said Herr Lang. "At least they don't need replacement parts."

As I was cleaning up the kitchen after dinner, Frau

Lang lingered, drying the dishes as I washed them. Once there was no one else with us I said, "Can you think of any way that I would be able to visit Salzburg?"

She looked at me oddly. "Why in heaven's name would you want to go to Salzburg?"

I gripped the dishrag in the hot soapy water. "When I came here, I was with a friend. He was taken off at Salzburg and he's working on the bridge there. I would love to see him, to make sure he's in good health."

"Maria, there's a war going on. This is not the time for visits."

I blinked back the hot tears that threatened to run down my cheeks, and I took a deep breath, trying to calm my anger. We worked in silence until the kitchen was cleaned.

Just before I left for the barn, Frau Lang said to me, "I know how hard it is to be separated from a loved one. If I can think of a way to get you to Salzburg, I will. Just don't hold your breath."

That night I dream I am running through the streets of Salzburg, shouting "Nathan, Nathan, where are you?" Suddenly, I find him, nearly buried under a rubble of rocks, his hands all cut and bleeding. "I'll help you," I tell him, tugging on both hands. "It's too late," he answers. "I've been buried alive . . ."

"Wake up, Maria!" Bianka's voice.

I jolted out of bed and looked around me. I was in the cow barn. There were no rocks; there was no Nathan. I wept.

Bianka's arms wrapped around me. "You were having a nightmare," she said. "You're fine; you're awake."

"It's Nathan," I said. "He's not fine. I've got to help him." I told her about what I asked of Frau Lang. I told her about what Otto had said about neutral countries.

"You don't have a plan though," said Bianka. "Even if you go to Salzburg, how will you find Nathan?"

"He works on the bridge."

"Hundreds must be building the bridge," said Bianka. "In all different shifts, and under watch. They probably stay at a work camp out of town. How would you even get to him? And even if you did, what then? Do you think you'd be able to stand there and have a conversation with him?"

"That's not helpful," I told her, wrapping my arms around my knees. "You're just giving me more things to have nightmares about."

"I'm talking about problems that need to be solved," said Bianka.

CHAPTER THIRTEEN
HITLER'S CHILD

Over the holidays, what with all the food and visitors, it was almost as if the war didn't exist for the Langs and Hubers, but when Otto went back to the Front, the entire household was plunged into sadness.

Sophie was back to her usual routine of leaving before the cows were milked and coming home after dinner, only to sleep, but then late one morning in mid-January, I encountered her in the kitchen, wearing her uniform and fussing about nervously, wiping down counters that were already clean. A suitcase was wedged between two of the kitchen chairs. When a sharp knock sounded on the kitchen door, she grinned. "Find *Mutter*," she said to me as she opened the door.

Gruppenführerin Winter stepped inside, and while Sophie took her coat and chattered about the weather, I went upstairs to get Frau Huber. She was exactly where

I knew she'd be: sitting on a wooden chair in Otto's bedroom, staring out the window. Today she was holding one of his old farm shirts up to her cheek. Once when I had gone up to get her she had dumped all of Otto's socks on the bed and was methodically sorting through them, putting them in some sort of special order. When I told her about the Gruppenführerin, she put down the shirt and said, "I'll be right down."

I set a plate of leftover swastika-shaped Linzer cookies on the kitchen table between Sophie and her unit leader. They were a bit on the stale side now and dare I admit that I had a mental image of Gruppenführerin Winter choking on one? But instead she bit in and chewed, and her face lit up. She turned to Sophie. "Did you make these yourself?"

"I did," said Sophie. "They're a lot of work, but I take pride in doing things properly."

In truth, Sophie had only watched them being made, but swastika cookies were not something I ever would have made out of free choice, so I was happy for her to take the credit. Frau Huber came downstairs as I poured boiling water into the teapot. I listened in on the conversation between Frau Huber and the group leader.

"Our girls have received a great honor," said Gruppenführerin Winter, taking another cookie.

"How wonderful," said Frau Huber in a voice that

did not convey any enthusiasm. "And what might this honor be?"

"Our unit has been selected to assist with a group of Aryan infants and children who have been evacuated to Czechoslovakia."

Frau Huber was silent for a long moment and when I set the teacups on the table, I noticed that her hands were in a white-knuckled clench on her lap. Finally, she answered, "That is indeed an honor. When will Sophie be leaving?"

"I'd like to take her with me now," said Gruppenführerin Winter.

Frau Huber inhaled sharply, but no words came out of her mouth.

"Don't worry, *Mut* . . . Frau Huber," said Sophie. "I've already packed my suitcase and I'm ready to go."

Frau Huber stood up so quickly that her kitchen chair nearly upended, but I caught it before it crashed to the floor. "Am I allowed to hug my daughter before she goes?" she asked. "Just this once?"

"You know that's not allowed," said the Gruppenführerin. "She's Hitler's child now." Her face softened just a bit and she said, "I'll let you shake her hand."

As Sophie and her group leader buttoned up their winter coats, Frau Huber stood by the door as if in a trance. I could tell that she was trying hard not to weep.

"Good-bye, Frau Huber," said Sophie, holding out her hand.

"Be brave, Sophie, and stay safe," said Frau Huber, clasping her daughter's hand in both of her own.

Sophie and the group leader walked out, and as the door closed behind them, Frau Huber's knees gave out. She crumpled to the floor and wept.

I didn't have to imagine what it was like for Frau Huber to be separated from her daughter because of war. After all, I was separated from everyone I loved.

And dare I say that Frau Huber was lucky? She wasn't Jewish: No one was hunting her down. She wasn't Ukrainian or Polish: No one was forcing her to work as a slave. Her son was still alive, and so were her daughter and husband. She didn't live in the war zone and she only had the Allies to worry about.

For me and my family and friends, it didn't matter who won the war: Both sides wanted us gone.

I put my arm around Frau Huber's waist and helped her to the table. I poured her a cup of tea and put an extra spoonful of sugar in it to give her strength.

As I cleaned cookie crumbs from the table and listened to Frau Huber weep, I couldn't help but wonder why *this* moment of leaving was the one that broke her. Sophie had been Hitler's child for years. You would have thought the separation was gradual enough that it wouldn't hurt so much. But who was I to judge? I had never been betrayed by a person I loved. Perhaps that hurt more than separation.

Or even death.

About a week after Sophie departed, Frau Huber asked us to box up Sophie's bedroom and to clean Otto's. It was rare for Bianka or me to be upstairs on our own, so as we carried up boxes, I whispered to Bianka, "I'm going to see if I can find my papers."

"Look for mine too," she said. "I'll keep an eye out for you."

It was Herr Lang who had taken my papers, so I figured he might have hidden them with his personal things. The bedroom he shared with Frau Lang was at the end of the hallway. The door creaked a bit as I pushed it open, and I was enveloped in the scent of lemon wax. The furniture was all gleaming dark wood. Pale light filtered through the curtained windows. As my eyes adjusted, I felt like I had stepped back into a time before the Nazis. There wasn't a single portrait of Hitler and no swastikas. A faded portrait of Franz Ferdinand, the assassinated Crown Prince of Austria, hung above the bed and there was a rosary on one of the night tables. The walls were adorned with old family photographs and it was interesting to see Frau Huber as a wild-haired child, and her parents when they were newly married.

Frau Lang had been telling the truth: She didn't believe in the Nazis and neither did her husband. They wanted the old Empire back. But even so, Herr Lang had kept my papers, and I needed to figure out where they were in case I ever needed to escape.

I opened the drawers of a tall dresser one by one, but each was filled with neat stacks of undergarments. There was a rolltop desk angled in the corner of the room and I checked the drawers there too, and while there were lots of documents, I couldn't find our identity papers. I pulled on the bottom drawer of the desk, but it wouldn't budge. It was probably locked. Is this where Herr Lang kept our papers?

Bianka popped her head in. "Have you found them?"

"I think they're in here," I said, pointing to the drawer. "But it's locked, so I can't be sure."

"Okay," said Bianka. "We may need a crowbar in an emergency, but at least we know where to look now."

Bianka had already started on Otto's room, so I reluctantly went to Sophie's, and as soon as I stepped in, I understood why Frau Huber wanted it cleared out. Sophie's entire wardrobe door was covered with newspaper clippings about Hitler. She also had a motif of hand-drawn swastikas decorating the frame of a photograph of her own family that hung on the wall. Even the books in her shelves made my stomach roil. There was a well-thumbed copy of *Mein Kampf* and various schoolbooks about Jews being evil or how to tell a Slav from an Aryan. As I loaded all this stuff into a cardboard box, I wondered how Sophie would react when she finally returned from Czechoslovakia. Would she be angry with her mother for clearing out her things?

Sophie had worn her uniform when she left with her unit leader, and I had assumed that she had packed her spare skirt and blouse as well, but when I opened her wardrobe and began sorting, there was an old uniform on the floor of the closet, shoved in the back behind her civilian clothing. I shook out the skirt and held it to my waist. It was too small for Sophie now, but I could easily wear it. The same was true of the blouse. I found a worn golden-brown outdoor jacket with the Nazi badge still on the left arm. I looked out into the hallway to make sure that no one was around and then I slipped the jacket on and stood in front of Sophie's mirror. It fit perfectly. I felt in the pocket and pulled out a key piece of the uniform—the black tie with its distinctive leather knot. Sophie had worn a uniform ever since she was ten years old. In all that time she had been taught to consider Hitler as her true parent and her mother as just Frau Huber. If I had been made to join the Hitler Girls at ten, would I be as awful as Sophie was now?

As I fastened the tie around my neck, I felt the power of the uniform wash over me. Maybe I didn't need my papers to get to Salzburg. Sophie was able to go anywhere she wanted and other Nazis treated her with respect. Civilians and foreign workers cowered in front of her, worrying that they could be reported if they questioned her. Did anyone ask her to show her papers when she went out in the Hitler Girls' uniform? Not likely. If I wore this uniform in public, would I have Sophie's power?

What if I borrowed this outfit and wore it to Salzburg? Could anyone really tell the difference between a Slav or an Aryan or a Jew if they were wearing a uniform? I looked in the mirror. I could pass. Maybe this was how I could get to Nathan.

"What in heaven's name are you doing, dressed like that?" Bianka stood in the doorway.

"You startled me," I said.

"Take that off." She crossed her arms. "The sight of you wearing that jacket and tie makes me ill."

I slipped off the tie and jacket and folded them up. Bianka took them from me, holding them away from her body as if she were holding a dead rat. She placed them in the cardboard box with the rest of Sophie's clothing.

"It's a good disguise," I said to her. "Who would question me if I was in Salzburg wearing that? I could find Nathan."

Bianka didn't say anything for a minute or more, but I could tell that she was thinking about it. "One big problem," she said. "As soon as you opened your mouth, they'd know you were a Slav. You don't speak German like an Austrian."

Bianka was right. I'd be caught for sure. "There has to be some way I can get to Nathan," I said.

"We'll keep thinking," said Bianka. "The important thing is that you don't get killed in the process."

CHAPTER FOURTEEN
LOVED ONES

The rest of January passed in a blur of daily chores. Bianka and I worked from dark until dark, caring for the cows and chickens, cleaning the barn, doing laundry, cooking for the family. Frau Huber gave us old sweaters to unravel and, with the reclaimed wool, we knitted socks and gloves for the Eastern Front. It made me angry to be helping my enemy. How I would have loved to put those socks and gloves in a box and send them to Mama and Krystia, or somehow get them to Nathan to keep him warm on that cold, high bridge. But then I thought of Otto in the harsh winter with Soviet bullets raining down. I had met him face-to-face and he had treated me like a human. Was Otto my enemy? He didn't believe in Hitler the way his sister did, yet he was in Hitler's army. And what about the Soviet army? They had killed my friends and family and that's who Otto was fighting. It was all so confusing.

I felt so powerless, but I was alive, and I had to consider that a small win. I could only hope and pray that Mama, Krystia, and Nathan were also alive.

At least both Nathan and I were in Austria and close to the Alps—protected from the Allied bombs that targeted German cities. And I was lucky to be on a farm where there was food.

On a bitterly cold morning in early February, Herr Lang stepped inside the barn, his face pale, as Bianka and I finished putting down fresh hay from the loft.

"Do either of you understand Russian well enough to translate?" he asked. "I've got the wireless set up in the kitchen tuned to Radio Moscow. They've been repeating a special bulletin all morning and we'd like to know what they're saying."

"I took Russian in school for two years under Soviet Occupation," I told Herr Lang.

"Maria, come, then," he said, opening the door wider.

Frau Huber and her mother were sitting at the kitchen table when we got there.

"Sit with us," said Herr Lang, as if we were all friends.

I sat down beside Frau Lang and listened to the tinny Russian voice on the radio:

The Red Army has now destroyed 330,000 German troops trapped in Stalingrad. This brings German army deaths to 500,000 since mid-November. As well, 91,000 troops have surrendered. This includes a field marshal, 23 generals, and thousands of officers.

I tried to take in the enormity of what was being said. The Nazis would have had to rampage through the countryside of Ukraine to get all the way to Stalingrad. The Soviets had already destroyed those same villages and towns as they retreated in 1941. How many army invasions could my homeland live through? Were Mama and Krystia safe? I had a mental image of Viteretz crushed under the weight of corpses from the two warring armies. All these people fighting and dying—for what?

I held my head in my hands and wept. It was all so devastating.

"What did he say?" Frau Huber reached out and gripped my hand.

Of course, Frau Huber and her parents weren't interested in what was happening with my family. They wanted to know about their own. I took a deep breath and said, "Let me listen to it one more time."

The tinny voice repeated the announcement, and I listened a second time. Everyone I loved was in the pathway of these armies, but Frau Huber's husband, Karl, had been right in Stalingrad over Christmas. Had Otto been sent back there too? Could both her son and husband have been killed at Stalingrad?

"Turn it off," I said.

Frau Lang twisted one of the dials until there was a firm click. Silence reigned.

I turned to Frau Huber. Slowly and carefully, I translated the announcement.

I expected Frau Huber to weep or scream, but she just sat there, her lips white and her eyes fixed on something in the distance. With great care, she stood. "I need to be alone."

After she left, Herr Lang said, "I don't think Otto was sent back there."

Frau Lang said, "Maybe Karl surrendered. He could still be alive."

I didn't want to add to their agony, so I kept my mouth shut, but I knew firsthand that to be killed by the Soviets or to be captured by them amounted to the same thing in the end. My cousin Josip suffered a long slow torture by the Soviets before they finally killed him. His injuries were so extensive that we could barely identify his body. Multiply this by the thousands of other civilians who were executed by the Soviets. But I had also seen the way the Nazis treated people—civilians and soldiers. During our escape, Nathan and I had seen a huge barbed wire enclo-sure full of ragged and starving Soviet soldiers, prisoners of war, corpses, and those barely alive all corralled together as if they were nothing but garbage.

I had never met Officer Huber, but for the sake of his family, I prayed that he was one of the lucky ones who wasn't captured or killed, but who somehow managed to get out of Stalingrad alive. As for Otto? I hoped that Herr Lang was right, that he hadn't been sent back to Stalingrad at all.

I wished the war would end and we could all go home.

With the fate of the Huber father and son unknown for weeks on end, a sadness hung over all of us as we did our daily chores. The radio was tuned to Radio Moscow each morning while the announcer read off the list of most recently identified German war dead. Frau Huber would sit motionless, holding her head in her hands as she stared at the tiny radio dials. When the announcer finished his daily list, she'd get up from the table and perform her tasks as if in a daze.

Other women whose sons or husbands were fighting would come to visit Frau Huber from time to time, and when that happened, they'd sit in the library with the door closed and converse in urgent whispers. Once, I walked past the library and heard whispering, so I eavesdropped.

"Stalin's troops are like cockroaches," said Frau Huber. "No matter how many of them Otto killed, he said they just kept swarming. I don't know how the Reich will ever take the Eastern Front with so many waves of Slavs willing to fight us."

"Don't worry," said an unfamiliar voice. "My Henrik told me Hitler's got a secret weapon up his sleeve."

"What's that?" asked Frau Huber.

"Poison gas," said the woman. "That'll clear those vermin out."

The words shocked me so much that I had to clamp my hand tightly over my mouth so they wouldn't hear me gasp. I tiptoed away, my heart pounding in my chest. Would the Nazis really drop poisoned gas on my homeland? I was a Slav, just like Stalin's troops. Did Frau Huber really think of me as a cockroach?

When I got to the cow barn, Bianka took one look at my face and asked me what was wrong, but I wouldn't tell her. It was bad enough for me to carry those words inside. I didn't want her to suffer with that as well. I tossed and turned that night, dreaming of mothers holding babies, old women dragging grandchildren away as a gray cloud of poison descended upon them.

February ended, and March began, but neither Otto's name nor Karl's was read out among the dead by Radio Moscow.

And then on the first day of April, a woman in Nazi Party uniform came to the door. I invited her in, my heart beating wildly, worried about what she might say. Frau Huber was in the laundry out back with Bianka, so I hurried to get her.

"Good morning, Frau," said the woman, bowing her head slightly. "You're Beatrice Huber, I take it, mother of Machine Gunner Otto Huber?"

Frau Huber's body swayed, and I was afraid that she would faint, so I took her elbow and tried to guide her to a chair, but she pushed me away. "I am Beatrice Huber," she replied, her hands clenched. "Do you have news of my son?"

"I do," said the group leader. "And it's good news. He is alive, but he has a serious head injury. He's been stabilized and is recovering at St. Johan's Hospital in Salzburg."

"Was my son injured in Stalingrad?" asked Frau Huber.

The woman looked momentarily puzzled, then shrugged, saying, "If he'd been in Stalingrad, I wouldn't be bringing you *good* news, now would I?"

Frau Huber muttered something. Her hand came up and she slapped the woman hard across the face. "My husband is at Stalingrad, you heartless witch. I've had no word if he is dead or alive."

The woman touched the red slap mark on her cheek and opened her mouth, then closed it again, staggering backward. "I—I . . . thank your family for their service."

As she stumbled down the steps, Frau Huber stood in the doorframe, hands on hips. "And don't you have the easy job, with all sorts of food and luxury, I'm sure. Thank you very much, for *your* service."

Herr Lang stood, aghast, at the foot of the steps. "My daughter didn't mean it," he said, taking the woman's elbow and walking her to her car. "She's had a shock . . ."

Frau Huber slammed the door and ran upstairs.

CHAPTER FIFTEEN
NATHAN'S BRIDGE

I felt for Frau Huber, truly I did, but the news of Otto being in Salzburg also filled me with hope. Frau Huber would visit her son in the hospital in Salzburg. She thought of me as a cockroach and so did her son, but I was a useful cockroach, wasn't I? Could I convince her to take me with her? Finally, there might be a way that I could get to Nathan.

"In the two years that I've been here, I've been allowed to go to the city just once, and that was only Innsbruck," said Bianka that night as we lay in our cowshed beds. "Salzburg is half a day away by train."

"But Frau Lang said she'd help me."

"Then you'll need to get Frau Lang to convince her daughter, won't you?"

It didn't take as much convincing as I anticipated. "St. Johan's Hospital is not far from the Salzburg Bridge," Frau

Lang said. "My daughter's friend Millicent runs a dress shop near there and so Beatrice has offered your services to her while the two of you stay at her house. You'll be busy, but hopefully, there will be some time for you to try to find your friend."

After all my worrying, it was going to be as easy as that to finally get to Nathan? My eyes filled with tears. "Thank you, Frau Lang."

"I told you I would try to help," she said. "And I trust that you won't abuse my faith in you."

We were packed up and ready to go by Saturday morning. Herr Lang gave Frau Huber my papers before we left, but he didn't look happy about it. "Give them back to me when you return," he said to her. "And she'd better return."

"I will come back to the farm," I said. "Thank you for trusting me."

A military officer glanced over Frau Huber's documents as we stood in line for the train at Innsbruck, but he spent several minutes examining mine. He looked me up and down with cool appraisal, then slapped the side of my face.

I stumbled with the shock of the slap.

"She has her P badge," said Frau Huber. "What has she done wrong?"

"Look for yourself," he said, pointing at the P on my heavy sweater. "It's not fully visible."

I looked down at the P. I had left the top of my sweater unbuttoned and so the collar hung down a fraction longer than usual, covering a tiny portion of the P, but it was still clearly visible.

I quickly buttoned up my sweater and straightened out the P. "I am sorry," I said, looking down at his boots.

"Consider this a favor," he said. "If you were to walk around like that in Salzburg, you could be shot."

"Thank you," said Frau Huber. "She's been on my farm since she got to the Ostmark, so it helps for her to know what is expected when we go to the big city."

The officer nodded and then motioned for us to get onto the train.

I picked up Frau Huber's two bulging satchels and we entered a train car that had seats and windows, unlike the freight car I had arrived in, where we had all been crushed together on the floor. Frau Huber motioned for me to sit beside her and that surprised me too, that an Aryan and Slav would sit side by side, but maybe the authorities understood that I was *her* Slav and she was keeping an eye on me, so they tolerated it. As the train sped toward Salzburg, I stared out the window, drinking in the sight of villages and countryside. After all these weeks being on the Huber farm, seeing a wide and ever-changing land-scape flash by was almost too much of a good thing. On my trip to the Ostmark, the only glimpses I got were as the doors of the freight car opened at each stop, and what I saw then was mostly train platforms, soldiers, and captured workers. Now I saw a peaceful landscape of rolling hills just beginning to turn green from the warmth of the spring and the huge mountains in the distance that protected us from Allied bombs. It was only when the train idled in towns along the way that I could see soldiers. They smiled and chatted with the civilians and this shocked me, at first. Back home in Viteretz, we civilians knew to keep our eyes cast to the ground whenever we passed a soldier because they were just as likely to shoot us as greet us. But then I remembered that the civilians in the Ostmark were Aryan, not Slav, so of course they weren't shot. We idled longer at one stop and I saw a group of ragged and thin foreign workers digging a ditch. The soldier who supervised wasn't smiling and chatting with them. His gun was poised, ready to shoot at the least sign of resistance. The sight sent a chill down my spine. Was Nathan working at gunpoint? Would I be able to find him? Was he still alive?

By the time we pulled into the Salzburg train station, it was late Saturday afternoon and I was grateful to step onto the platform to stretch my legs. Frau Huber opened her purse and took out a map. "My friend's house is three kilometers from here," she said. "And we can get most of the way there by tram."

I rested Frau Huber's two heavy satchels at my feet once we found a vacant bench to sit on in the electric tram. As it rumbled through the city streets, I looked out the window and marveled at the perfect condition of the buildings. In my hometown of Viteretz, many buildings had been destroyed, some by the Soviets and others by the Nazis. I thought of all the civilians who must have died as both armies rampaged on to Stalingrad. Yet here in Salzburg, you'd hardly know there was a war. Yes, there were Nazi soldiers in uniform sitting on the tram with us, but they seemed relaxed. What jarred me was seeing Aryan women in expensive dresses who chatted and smiled among themselves. You'd never guess that their husbands, fathers, and sons were on the battlefield fighting for their lives.

The tram approached a grocery store with plentiful displays of meat and fruit in the window. As we passed by, I read a hand-printed notice that had been taped to the window: NO DOGS OR FOREIGN WORKERS ALLOWED.

That sign made me burn with anger. All this food had been stolen from people who lived in the war zone like me. And *we* were the dogs?

I steadied Frau Huber's satchels as the tram slowed down in front of a palace with a huge manicured garden.

A few moments later, it stopped in front of the stately old buildings of Salzburg University. As I watched a couple of students get on the tram, I wondered how people who seemingly had so much culture and education could be so cruel to their fellow humans. We passed a triple-domed Catholic church and then the tram stopped again, this time in front of a huge pale pink house.

Frau Huber looked up at the house and then checked something on her map.

"Have we arrived?" I asked.

"No," said Frau Huber. "That's where Mozart lived."

Out the window, I spotted a ladies' store named Millicent's Beautiful Dresses. My heart sank as I noticed the NO DOGS OR FOREIGN WORKERS sign taped to the bottom of her display window.

"Is that your friend's store?" I asked.

Frau Huber nodded. "We're almost at our stop."

The tram turned sharply, so I clutched the luggage once again, and then it shuddered to a stop at the foot of a bridge.

I grabbed the two bags and stepped onto the street behind Frau Huber. We walked past Millicent's and across the bridge, and I stopped in shock at the sight down the river. A series of concrete structures jutted out of the water like huge broken teeth. The two at the opposite side of the river were connected by a network of metal cables. Above them, an impossibly tall mechanical crane was lowering a long steel beam into a nest of cables between the two concrete structures. There were four workers balanced on the steel beam, guiding it, and others poised on the concrete structure below, ready to steady it. On solid land beside the bridge a few guards watched, their guns pointed toward the workers. This was what it meant to build the Salzburg Bridge? One false step would plunge a worker to his death and one wrong move would get the worker shot. Is this what Nathan had been doing all these months? I squinted and stared but couldn't recognize any of the workers as Nathan, but I was close to finding him now.

Frau Huber grabbed one of the satchels and guided me by the elbow across the bridge, and then we turned left, walking along the Salzach River toward Nathan's bridge. I couldn't pull my eyes away from the ragged boys dangling in the air as we passed by. Half a block later, Frau Huber stopped at the entrance to an alleyway. "Here we are," she said. "Millicent's house is number 17."

The narrow cobblestoned street reminded me of the Old Town in Lviv with its tall pastel-washed houses built so close together that they touched. When we got to number 17, Frau Huber knocked. The door opened wide and a woman with pale hair swirled into a high bun welcomed us into a spacious entryway. "Beatrice, it's so good to see you," Millicent said, giving Frau Huber a kiss on each cheek.

Her eyes slid over me and she pointed down the hallway to an opened door. "You can put those bags in the guest room. Anna will show you to the servants' quarters."

I walked down the hallway, stepped inside the guest room, and set the satchels on the floor. In addition to the expected bed and night table, there were packages tied with string stacked up against one of the walls and a metal garment rack hung with half a dozen elegant dresses. I thought back to that box Officer Huber had sent before Christmas—and the blood Frau Huber made me remove from the wedding dress. Just that one dress had given me nightmares. How many dead people did these loot boxes represent?

A girl about my age stepped into the bedroom, drying her hands on an apron. "I'm Anna," she said, holding out a hand. "What's your name?"

"Maria," I said, shaking her hand. There was a letter P stitched onto the front of her dress. "Are you Polish or Ukrainian?"

"Ukrainian."

"Me too."

She gestured for me to follow her to the kitchen at the

end of the hallway. Once we were out of earshot, Anna said, "Where are you from?"

"Viteretz, not far from Lviv. And you?"

Anna smiled. "I'm from Ternopil," she said. "We're practically neighbors."

"How long have you been here?" I asked.

"A few weeks," she said. Her smile vanished. "Mama sent me out to stand in the bread line, but it was a trick to capture us. Frau Schwartz doesn't beat me, though, and the work isn't too hard. I'm luckier than most."

"What do you do?" I asked.

"There are house chores, but mostly I change the labels on the dresses Officer Schwartz sends from Paris stores," she said.

"So those dresses aren't collected from people being executed?" I asked.

"They raid the stores, but the French are considered Aryan."

"But if they're new, why bother changing the labels?"

"Hitler doesn't think French fashion is patriotic," said Anna. "Besides, some of the French designers are Jewish, so I remove the tags and replace them with ones that say *Millicent's.*"

"And this makes them acceptable?" I asked.

"Frau Schwartz says they're very popular with officers' wives and others who have lots of money."

I thought back to the healthy-looking people on the tram and the chattering students from the university. Here the stores were filled with food and luxury items. It was how I imagined Auntie Stefa's Toronto. "It seems the war hardly exists here except to supply Aryans with stolen food, clothing, and workers."

"That's how I see it too," said Anna.

I sat down and looked around the kitchen, taking in the two sinks, the two sets of cupboards, and side-by-side worktables. It hit me all at once: This house was stolen too—from a Jewish family. I had been in Nathan's kitchen many times and it was just like this, with two of everything because they separated their meat and dairy in the kosher tradition.

"This house was Jewish," I said.

Anna nodded. "You're right. I overheard Frau Schwartz talk about it. Salzburg only had about a hundred Jews to begin with and now they're all executed."

And yet Nathan—if he still lived—was no more than a stone's throw away. What would the Nazis do if they found out they'd missed one Jew?

"Come with me," Anna said, startling me out of my thoughts. "I'll show you where you sleep."

I followed her up to a stuffy attic at the top of the house. The space was cluttered with damaged antique furniture, ripped bedding, and winter coats that smelled of sweat. Anna had cleared a space in the middle of the floor and had made a nest with old clothing and blankets.

"It doesn't look all that appealing," said Anna. "But it's cozy and warm, and there's plenty of room for both of us."

"I usually sleep in a cow barn," I said. "This is an improvement."

I followed Anna back downstairs, unpacked Frau Huber's bags, then assisted Anna with setting out dinner. As the two old friends ate and chatted, Anna and I went back upstairs to the attic.

"When do we eat?" I asked.

"Frau Schwartz feels that it's patriotic to leave no waste," said Anna. "She doesn't allot us any food at all, but we are allowed to eat any table scraps that are left over."

Her words shouldn't have stunned me, but they did. "Back at the farm," I said, "even the dog gets more than just scraps."

"I've heard that farms are the best place to be," said Anna. "You're lucky you were assigned to one."

"Frau Huber and her parents treat me as well as they can," I said. "And for that I'm grateful. But I'm also excited about being in Salzburg."

"Why?" she asked.

"I have a friend who was taken to work on the bridge, and I haven't seen him since we were split up months ago."

Anna's eyes lit up. "Perfect timing," she said. "Tomorrow is Sunday and it's the only time slave laborers are given time off. The entire town square fills up with them, so if you want to find your friend, tomorrow is the day to do it."

That night I went to bed hungry because Frau Huber didn't realize the food rules of the house and she ate up every last scrap. That didn't matter though. All I could think of was seeing Nathan.

CHAPTER SIXTEEN
WATCHING

On Sunday morning, I assisted Anna with breakfast and cleaning up, and I got something to eat too, because Frau Huber must have realized that her friend didn't feed us. I buttoned up my sweater, making sure that the P was clearly visible, and asked Frau Huber for my papers so I could go to the town square with Anna.

As she handed them to me, Frau Schwartz snatched them back. "She's done no work for me yet, Beatrice. Why would I give her time off?"

Frau Huber looked like she was about to argue with her friend, but she must have reconsidered. "Be industrious this week and you'll get your day off next Sunday."

Next Sunday? Would we even be in Salzburg next Sunday? What if, after all this planning, I still didn't get to see Nathan? Her words filled me with panic. I forced myself to breathe slowly and pasted on a smile. "Yes, Frau Huber," I said.

While Anna went to the town square, I was given the disgusting job of handwashing Frau Schwartz's delicate undergarments, and as I scrubbed the items in cold soapy water, I had to be careful not to let the calluses on my fingers catch at the fragile material. I used to help Mama with the washing too, and thinking of us working side by side, elbow-deep in suds, made my throat catch in sorrow. What was Mama doing right now? Did she think of me as much as I thought of her? How I wished I could be back home, helping Mama with her chores instead of washing these impractical fancy things for mean Frau Schwartz.

The next day while Frau Huber visited Otto at the hospital, Anna and I hunched over Frau Schwartz's kitchen table and picked away at silk stitches. My shoulders ached, and my head throbbed from the tedious work, but it was a job that I was good at, and I took pride in a job well done. By the end of the day, the old silk labels that identified the real creators of these lovely gowns fluttered around Anna and me like autumn leaves.

Frau Schwartz brought home a dress from one of her clients that evening. "This needs to be fixed by tomorrow afternoon," she said, taking a gauzy pink dress from the garment bag and fanning it out on the kitchen table. There was a hole at the hem the size and shape of a woman's spike heel.

"Beatrice told me how good you are at fixing delicate fabric," said Frau Schwartz. "It's a happy coincidence that I have you here."

I took the damaged material in my hands and examined it; I realized that it wasn't as bad as I had initially thought. The pencil-thin heel had miraculously not punctured the sheer material but had shifted the weave and deposited a smudge of dirt. "I can repair this," I said. "Do you want me to do it now?"

Frau Schwartz looked at her wristwatch and frowned. "It's too late. I have some friends coming over for a card game after dinner, and I'll need you both to be serving."

"It should take me an hour, maybe two," I said. "I'll start on it as soon as breakfast is cleared away in the morning."

"That will be perfect," said Frau Schwartz. "Anna can bring it to the store once you've fixed it."

"I could bring it myself, if you like," I replied, trying not to sound too eager. Finally, an opportunity to find Nathan!

"Anna can do it," said Frau Schwartz. "She's done it before and knows the way."

Her answer made me want to scream, but I took a deep breath and nodded.

That night in our attic, Anna said, "Tell me about your friend."

In whispers, I told her everything, about how we had been fast friends since we were young, about the ghetto and his mother's death, and the false papers we were able to get for him. "We fled together after he survived his execution," I said. "We thought we could hide here in plain sight." I brushed a tear from my face with the back of my hand. "And it almost worked, but we got separated."

"Maybe I can find Nathan tomorrow," she said. "I pass right by the bridge on the way back from the store. I can ask around."

"Thank you," I said, hugging Anna. "Ask around for Bohdan Sawchuk. That's what his papers say."

After Anna and I cleared away the breakfast dishes the next morning, I spread the damaged dress out on the table. As I gently soaped the damaged spot, I was grateful to be removing just dirt, not blood. As the fabric got sudsy, the dirt loosened and the threads became pliable. I positioned the slippery wet patch on top of a china plate, and with two sewing needles I carefully teased the threads back to their original position. Each bit of gauzy thread could only be shifted a tiny bit with each tug or else it could break or fray. My shoulders and neck ached from concentrating so hard, but I was pleased with the result.

"You can't even tell it was damaged," said Anna, holding the bottom of the dress up to the light for a better look. "I'll put a bit of starch on the spot and iron it for you."

After Anna left to take the dress to the store, I was anxious, wondering whether Anna would find Nathan, wishing that I could go outside myself. I was also nervous about being in that house on my own again. Every squeak and footstep from outside made me jumpy.

But also, being alone gave me time to think about what I was doing and those were not comfortable thoughts. Here I sat in a stolen house, preparing stolen dresses for Nazi women.

I thought of the ruined items in the attic and wondered if Frau Schwartz had moved into the house with all the evidence of violence still on display. From what I knew of her so far, it probably wouldn't have bothered her. She was like a vulture, feasting on the dead.

Suddenly, the front door opened, then heavy footsteps. Too heavy for Anna.

I felt like hiding, but I was frozen on my chair.

Into the kitchen walked an elderly man with a swastika armband. He had to be the local Blockleiter. Of course they'd have Blockleiters in Salzburg too. This man looked too old to fight, which was probably why he was given this job instead.

"*Heil* Hitler, Blockleiter," I said, stumbling to my feet, my eyes cast down to the floor.

"You're the Slav helping Millicent for a while, aren't you?" he asked.

"Yes, Blockleiter," I said. "My name is Maria Fediuk."

"Show me your work." His voice sounded bored.

The kitchen table was a mess of labels, needles, and thread, but a garment rack of finished gowns stood to one side and it was half full. Hopefully, he'd see that as evidence that I was working hard. The Blockleiter nodded, and without another word, he turned and left. I collapsed back down onto my chair and took a deep breath, knowing that whatever I did and wherever I went, I was being watched.

Anna came home not long after the Blockleiter's visit and her eyes were lit up with excitement. "I just spoke to someone who knows your Bohdan," she said.

"He's alive?"

"He is," she said. "And he's still working at the bridge, but today his unit was excavating rock out of town."

"Will I be able to see him on Sunday?" I asked.

Anna nodded. "I told his friend that you'd meet him at the fountain in the town square at one o'clock. He works

Sunday morning, but gets the afternoon off. I'll take you there, so you won't get lost."

"Thank you, Anna," I said, giving her a big hug. "I'm so excited I can hardly think straight."

"Just do good work for Frau Schwartz all this week so she'll let you have the time off."

CHAPTER SEVENTEEN
OSTERIA TYROL

The minutes and hours dragged on for the rest of the week, but I made a point of working hard and keeping a smile on my face so that Frau Schwartz would have no complaints.

When it was finally Sunday morning, preparing breakfast seemed to take forever, and so did serving it and cleaning up afterward. I was about to eat my half of the bit of sausage, bread crusts, and leftover cheese, but then thought of Nathan. How much was he getting to eat? I put on my sweater, buttoned it up to the top so the P showed clearly, then put the scraps of food in my pocket to share with Nathan when I saw him.

Frau Huber called me into her bedroom and handed me my papers. She lifted her hand and brought it to my face. I flinched, but all she did was brush a piece of my hair out of my eyes. "Be mindful of the police," she said.

Maybe she was only concerned about losing a good worker, but that's not what it felt like. It was almost as if she cared for me like a fellow human being. I resisted the urge to hug her, or even to offer a handshake. I was a Slav and she was an Aryan, after all, and she said herself she thought Slavs were cockroaches. I settled on a polite nod and said, "Thank you, Frau Huber, I'll be on my best behavior."

As I stepped out of the house behind Anna, I could barely contain my excitement. I was free, if only for a short while, and in just a few hours I would see Nathan!

We walked up to the corner and turned left onto the main street that followed the river. Because it was Sunday, there were lots of people walking about. I stepped onto the sidewalk, but Anna grabbed my elbow and pulled me onto the road, and I almost got hit by a car.

"Why did you do that?" I asked, feeling shaken.

"We can't walk on the sidewalk if an Aryan is on it," she said.

We walked on the edge of the road, trying not to get in the way of the Aryans or the cars passing in front of Nathan's bridge. I would have loved to stop and look for him. But Anna took me by the elbow and guided me away.

"You'll see him soon enough," she said. "There's some-place else I want to be."

We walked along the river and across the next bridge to the old part of town, passing Millicent's Beautiful Dresses and briefly stopping at Mozart's pink house to admire it, although to me, the only notable thing about all the buildings in Salzburg was that they were untouched by war. We continued down the street, then stopped at the T-intersection. Across the road at the top of the T was the magnificent triple-domed Catholic church that I had seen on the tram ride when we arrived in Salzburg. The doors were now wide open, and a priest paused on the step, greeting worshippers as they entered. I stood beside Anna, mesmerized by the sight. I would have loved to cross the road and go inside to pray and be enveloped in the familiar scent of incense and wrapped within beloved hymns. It would be so comforting. I knew that the Roman Catholic Mass wasn't quite the same as our Ukrainian Catholic Divine Liturgy but it was close enough.

"I'd love to go in," said Anna, giving my hand a squeeze.

"But we're not allowed, are we?"

"I know a girl who hid her P badge and went in anyway," said Anna. "But if she were caught, I hate to think what they would do to her."

"Can we stand right here and listen?" I asked.

"I know a better place," said Anna, and she led me to a small park close by.

We knelt side by side on the grass facing the church and held our hands in prayer. The last of the worshippers stepped in, but the priest paused and smiled when he noticed us. He looked right at us and made a sign of the cross in the air. Instead of closing the door completely, he propped it open a bit with the doorstop. I like to think he left it open so we could listen, and his kindness nearly made me weep.

We stayed there kneeling for the full hour, and although I didn't understand the Latin, the rhythm of the prayers and hymns soothed me.

No policeman came up to us for that full hour, and when the Mass ended and the doors opened up again, my legs were numb and I could barely stumble to my feet. For the first time in a long time I felt like my old self—not a Slav, not a slave, but Maria: daughter, sister, friend.

"That was almost as good as being inside the church," I said to Anna.

The town square with the fountain was a block away, and even though the clock had just rung twelve, I was anxious to get there in case Nathan got off early.

The square was a crush of foreign workers and the babble of many languages filled the air. I stood and listened, recognizing Ukrainian, Polish, Russian, French. Young people milled about, clustering in groups, arguing, singing, bartering. There were policemen with swastikas on their armbands in the area too, but they just seemed to be watching.

A group of girls wearing P badges sat cross-legged in a circle on the grass. "Anna," one of them called. "Come and sit with us."

Anna guided me over to the group and we both sat down. They were playing a game, where one girl sang a line from a popular song and the girl sitting next to her had to continue it. If you didn't know the words, you could make them up. The results were quite hilarious.

"Stay with your friends," I whispered into Anna's ear after the first round ended. "I'm going to go wait by the fountain."

"Good luck," she said. "I'll meet up with you later."

I leaned against the fountain and watched the mayhem around me, reveling in this one small stretch of freedom amid so many days and weeks of work. The warmth of the sun felt good on my face, and I was tempted to unbutton my sweater but didn't want to risk hiding a portion of my badge.

I scanned the crowd, pausing to look at the faces of boys who were Nathan's height or build, but there were so many of them and they all looked the same—scruffy, dirty, thin. I was lost in my thoughts. The clock bell gonged. It was one o'clock.

I stood on my tiptoes and scanned the crowd, anxious to get a glimpse of Nathan as he approached the fountain, but I couldn't see anyone who looked like him. And then I heard someone make the call of the falcon: *kak kak kak*. My heart soared. That had to be Nathan, using the secret call that we'd used in the Underground. I hadn't seen him, but he had seen me.

And then I felt a light tap on my shoulder. I turned. Nathan.

His eyes looked too big for his face and his hair had grown shaggy, but the smile was the same. He was my dear friend Nathan. "I've missed you so much, *Bohdan*," I said in Ukrainian. I desperately wanted to hug him, to weep with relief, but that would draw attention.

He took one of my hands and his palm felt like cracked dry leather. He tightened his fingers around my knuckles and squeezed. I nearly winced. Building that bridge had made him strong. "I missed you too," he said.

I longed to stop time, to just visit and talk about unimportant things like we used to before the war. But there were more important things than having a social visit. I had to save Nathan's life.

"I need to tell you something," I whispered.

He led me to a spot where there were fewer people and bent his head down so his ear was close to my lips and his shaggy hair tickled my nose. "Get to Switzerland," I said. "It's neutral."

He tilted his head and looked at me quizzically. "How?"

I pulled him closer again and whispered in his ear, "Salzburg to Innsbruck. Follow the tracks or hide on the train. Innsbruck station is a hub. The tracks west from Innsbruck that go through the mountains will take you to safety."

"Come with me," he said, brushing a stray hair from my cheek.

"I'm safe on the farm. You're not safe here."

"How far is Thaur from Innsbruck?" he asked.

"Walking distance," I said.

"We could escape together."

His words caught at my throat. Nathan was like the brother I never had. To be with him again, someone to laugh with and to trust. It would be like old times. And how I would love to escape to a free country, where we could live in peace without Nazis or Soviets breathing down our necks. But now was not the time. Didn't Nathan realize that he might be the last Jew alive in Salzburg? He had to get out. Traveling together would only complicate that. And what about Krystia and Mama? I had to get back to them.

"What are you thinking?" asked Nathan.

I looked into his face, willing him to read my mind. I couldn't possibly tell him all that I was thinking. We were in a public place.

Nathan's eyes focused on something behind me. "Let's walk for a bit," he said. "Police."

We strolled side by side with my hand on his elbow and I suddenly felt sad. I had been looking forward to this day for so long but soon it would be over, and I wasn't sure if I had made Nathan understand how urgent it was for him to escape.

A policeman came up to us and said, "I saw you whispering. That's not allowed."

"Yes, Officer," I said, bowing my head.

We walked around the square and I tried to make it look like I was interested in the antics of the other young people who were enjoying their day off, but they could have all disappeared and I wouldn't have noticed. I savored these moments with Nathan.

When the policeman was busy with someone else, I asked Nathan, "How do they treat you?"

"We sleep in a camp on beds of dirty straw," he said. "They beat us often and feed us rarely. You?"

"There's food to eat on a farm," I said. "And I've only been badly beaten once, by the daughter, and she's gone to Czechoslovakia."

"I wish I was there with you."

"Me too." I reached into my pocket and pulled out the end of cheese from breakfast. "This is for you."

He broke it in half and gave one piece back to me. "I know you," he said. "You haven't eaten today, have you?"

That made me smile.

"One, two, three . . . we'll eat together," he said, holding his piece between his teeth and giving me a goofy grin.

That made me laugh. It was so good to be with Nathan again.

Suddenly, I felt a firm grip on my arm. "What are you laughing about?" It was the policeman.

"About . . . about eating cheese," I said, trying to contain my giggles.

"I don't think so," said the policeman. "You're laughing at me, aren't you? I saw you glancing over my way. You're probably laughing at all Austrians."

Nathan's face went still and I could feel my heart pound. "No, Officer," said Nathan. "Maria gave me some cheese to eat."

I pulled out a crust of bread from my pocket. "I saved this to share with my friend," I told him.

"Show me your papers," he said.

I took them out of my pocket and showed him. Nathan handed his to the policeman as well. The officer glanced at Nathan's and gave them back, but he held onto mine.

"You're assigned to the Huber farm in Thaur, yet you're here in Salzburg," he said. "That's very suspicious."

"Frau Huber is visiting her son at the hospital," I said. "He's a machine gunner and was injured. She brought me here with her and I'm helping her friend Millicent Schwartz." I pointed in the direction of the dress store.

"I don't believe you."

The policeman's words filled me with dread. He could shoot me on the spot if he wanted, and he could kill Nathan as well—and all because we made a joke about a piece of cheese.

I turned and saw Nathan standing there, his face rigid with alarm. I did not want him to do something stupid and brave like try to intervene. I had to stay calm so Nathan would stay calm. I took a deep breath and willed my heart to stop its pounding.

"Be safe," I called to Nathan in as steady a voice as I could manage.

He nodded, his eyes locked onto mine.

The policeman roughly dragged me through the square and deeper into the old town until we reached a restaurant called the Osteria Tyrol. He opened the door and pulled me in.

It was a restaurant full of chatting, eating, laughing Austrians, but they all went silent and stared at us as he ushered me through the tables and stopped in front of one of them.

To my horror, there was Frau Schwartz in her Sunday best, sitting with a couple of other women plus several Nazi officers in uniform, their medals glittering in the electric light.

"Tante Millie," said the policeman. "This Slav pig says she works for you, but her papers don't show that."

"Fritz, you've surprised me," said Frau Schwartz, her eyes darting from her table guests' impatient glances to the policeman—her nephew. "Maria is working for me. Has she done something wrong?"

"She was laughing at Austrians," he said.

One of the officers at the table took a sip from his coffee cup and set it back down with a clatter. "She should be beaten," he said.

"Hans," said Frau Schwartz in a soothing voice to the officer who wanted me beaten. "This girl is quite useful. In fact, she was the one who salvaged your daughter's party dress."

The officer's eyebrows rose in surprise. "You don't want her beaten?"

"Not today."

Frau Schwartz's voice was so calm and neutral, and it

made me wonder what she was really thinking. Would she get in trouble for defending a Slav? I never would have judged her as kind or brave, but she had just proven me wrong.

She turned to the policeman and said, "Fritz, do me a favor and accompany the Slav back to my house. That way we'll know she won't get into any more trouble."

"I'll do that, Tante," said the policeman.

I could feel my face get hot with embarrassment as we exited the restaurant and walked back through town. The policeman kept a firm grip on my elbow the whole way.

He didn't say a word until we got to Frau Schwartz's door, but I could tell that he was angry. "If I catch you laughing at Austrians again, I'll shoot you on sight."

I nodded in response. He turned and stomped away. I tumbled into the house and closed the door behind me, my knees like jelly.

That night, as I curled up to sleep, I tried to sort out my feelings. Yes, I would have liked to visit longer with Nathan and it was devastating to think that if he escaped, we'd never see each other again.

But I had seen him with my own eyes! He was alive and he was strong.

And I had accomplished what I had come for: I had

told Nathan about the escape route. Now I just had to pray that he'd take my advice.

I hugged my knees close to my chest and felt the thrill of a job well done. But more than that, I had hope.

Hope that Nathan might take my advice and escape. Hope that Nathan might *live*.

Hope that we might somehow find each other after the war.

And hope that Frau Schwartz's unexpected kindness wasn't a solitary incident.

CHAPTER EIGHTEEN
OTTO

I didn't get to see Nathan again because we went back to the farm a few days later. Otto was released from the hospital, and Frau Schwartz arranged for a military car to take us all home.

Anna carried one of Frau Huber's satchels to the curb outside and I carried the other, plus Otto's.

I gave Anna a big hug as we waited for the car to arrive. "I'll miss you."

"Me too," she said, brushing a tear from her eye. "Come see me in Ternopil after the war."

"I will."

Just then, a long black car with a small swastika flag on either side of the hood pulled up to the curb. A fresh-faced soldier hopped out. "I'm taking Beatrice and Otto Huber plus one Slav back to their farm in Thaur," he said.

"Yes, Officer," I said. "I'm the worker, and they're just inside the door."

He put the luggage in the trunk and ordered me to sit in the front seat of the car. "And you"—he pointed to Anna—"tell the Hubers that I'm here."

Frau Huber guided Otto into the back seat. He leaned back and closed his eyes.

Once we got out of Salzburg, the road was congested with refugees and slave workers on foot, in addition to farm wagons and military vehicles. But people hurried to get out of the way as soon as they noticed the swastika flags on our car. We sped down the road and the landscape changed so quickly that it almost made me dizzy.

A few hours later, we turned off the road and into the Huber laneway. I looked out into the fields and saw that they had been seeded while we were gone. How was that even possible?

When we got to the house, the car stopped, and we got out. Max greeted Otto, nearly knocking him over, and then it was my turn. As he covered my face with wet dog kisses, I thought back to how terrified I was the first time I had encountered Max. Now he was like an old friend.

I found Bianka in the laundry, her hair a cloud of curls

from the steamy water. Her face lit up when she saw me, and she dried her hands on her apron and ran over.

"I'm so glad that you're back," said Bianka, enveloping me in a hug. She held me at arm's length and frowned. "You've lost weight."

"Foreign workers aren't fed much in the city," I said. "But that doesn't matter, because I talked to Nathan. He's alive!"

She laughed and grabbed me by the waist. We twirled around the laundry room in a fast polka. "I am so happy for you!" she said. "This gives me hope that one day I may find Gustave."

Later that night, as we settled down to sleep, I asked her, "Who seeded the fields?"

"The Blockleiter arranged for a truckload of foreign workers to come here for a few days before being shipped off to a work camp farther north," she said.

When I closed my eyes, I had an image of those unfortunate souls who were treated like animals. Just like me, they were controlled and sent where they were needed. The whole country seemed to run on slaves.

May turned into June and the heavy chores of milking, barn cleaning, and kitchen work blended together in one exhausting blur. Bianka and I never complained though. We knew we were the lucky ones when it came to foreign workers. All over the Ostmark, new concentration camps had opened up to deal with all the civilians on the Eastern Front who were captured and sent to the Reich as slaves. I heard Frau Huber whisper to her mother that she heard there were now fifty slave camps in Austria.

Even with all these new slaves, Frau Huber wasn't given any more permanent workers for the farm. It was a war, after all, and Hitler was most interested in making bombs, bullets, and guns.

Farmers still had to deliver produce, though, or Hitler's soldiers would starve. Bianka and I couldn't do it on our own, so Frau Huber leased dozens of people from a slave camp one day to come and weed the fields. These starved and ragged workers were accompanied by soldiers from the camp, or should I say sadists from the camp? Once, I watched with my own eyes as a soldier beat a prisoner to death because the man fainted while pulling weeds in the hot sun. I know Herr Lang saw it too, and while he looked troubled by the incident, he didn't report the soldier.

When Otto first got home he couldn't sleep in his old room because the morning light was too bright, even with the blackout curtains. We set up a bed for him in the library because it was the only room in the house without windows. When I took him a cup of tea or something to eat, he would be sitting in the darkness, his eyes closed, and his forehead wrinkled in pain. I felt so bad for Frau Huber. Her son had survived, and he was home, but he was far from well.

For much of the summer, Otto spent most of his time closed in the library with all the lights off, but as the weeks progressed, he slowly improved. Sometimes I would see him before dawn sitting by himself at the outdoor table in front of the farmhouse. Once, when I got up in the middle of the night for a drink of water, I was startled to see him wandering in the open hilly meadow under the moonlight.

Toward the end of summer, Otto occasionally came outside in the daytime, but he always wore a broad-brimmed hat to keep the glare of the sun from his eyes.

CHAPTER NINETEEN
A THOUSAND TONS OF BOMBS

I would have loved to have nothing to do but sleep and eat and wander around at night, but instead I was drowning in the grind of work, work, work.

A thousand tons of Allied bombs fell on German cities the summer of 1943, and as houses were destroyed and German civilians became homeless, they fled to the Austrian Alps. The Blockleiter ordered Frau Huber to prepare for an influx. "You should see Innsbruck right now," she said, helping herself to one of the freshly baked biscuits that was cooling on the kitchen counter. "Hotels and boarding houses are full. Restaurants can't keep up with the demand."

"We could clear out a portion of the cow loft for sleeping," said Frau Huber. "My son weatherproofed the barn last Christmas, so it would be comfortable."

"These are Aryans, not Slavs," said the Blockleiter, taking a small bite from her biscuit and swallowing it. "They will stay in the house."

Bianka and I cleaned the bunk room, which was bright and airy, with enough beds to hold a dozen people comfortably. The first to arrive were three women from Munich. Magda, Angela, and Claire arrived by car unannounced. Frau Huber took them through the house, pointing out the dining room, the bathroom, and Otto's library. She stopped in front of the dormitory and said, "This is where you'll sleep."

"This looks like it's for servants," said Claire. "I'd like my own room, please."

"You can stay in the bunk room, or you can go somewhere else," said Frau Huber firmly.

"There isn't any other place to go," said Claire.

"Well, then, I'll get my girls to bring in your luggage."

We set their suitcases in the hallway and the three women counted out their extra ration cards and cash and placed it all into Frau Huber's waiting palm. And then they got into their car and went on a drive through the countryside.

The women came back a few hours later, chattering happily among themselves. "We've got fruit and cheese and coffee," said Angela, handing Frau Huber a net bag.

"The storekeeper wasn't going to let us have this, but I insisted."

These women with their fancy outfits were high society, and they expected to have everything done for them. They treated Bianka and me like we were their servants, and they treated the Huber family nearly the same way.

On the radio, we kept hearing that all German women were to be working for the war, but as far as I could tell, all that these women did was go to Innsbruck for black-market shopping, and gossip among themselves. From overhearing snippets of their conversation, I was certain that all three were married to high-ranking Nazi officials.

The most annoying of the women was Magda Schmitz, who said to me, "Do you want to see a surprise?" She opened her purse and a yappy white dog jumped out, startling me so badly that I nearly fainted.

"Zelda won't hurt you," said Magda, scratching the rat-like creature affectionately between the ears.

The dog went everywhere with Magda, and it even sat on her lap during meals. Magda never cleaned up after Zelda, so I would find bits of dog poo and pee puddles all over the house.

Zelda drove Max crazy. Whenever they were in the yard at the same time, they'd yip themselves into a frenzy.

Each day, Magda wore a different dress with matching jewelry and she'd traipse around the house, scratching the wooden floors with her high heels. While we all worked from morning until night, Magda complained that there was nothing to do.

Claire and Angela weren't much better. They played cards in the dining room for hours on end, talking and laughing as they did so. Like Magda, they wore expensive dresses, but they had maybe half a dozen outfits each. Magda seemed to have an endless supply. I wondered if her husband was stationed in Paris like Frau Schwartz's.

Once, as I was setting down a plate of cookies for the German women, I caught a bit of their conversation.

"My town house is completely gone," said Magda, with a deep sigh. Zelda was asleep on her lap. "I was at our country house when it happened, thank God. Otherwise, I would have been flattened."

"I would have just as soon stayed in Munich," said Angela Zimmer, a thin-lipped woman who was admiring her long red fingernails. "But my husband insisted that I leave. He couldn't stand the humiliation of having me ordered to work in an office or do some ghastlier thing for the war effort."

"We are doing our part, with the sacrifices we're making," said Claire. Her hair was piled in elaborate waves on top of her head and she wore a gauzy blue dress with flowers painted on it. "The restaurants don't have good food anymore, and the theaters only show propaganda. I can't even find French wine in the stores anymore."

As I set down a pot of tea, Claire glanced my way and grimaced. "These foreigners are overrunning the Reich."

"I know what you mean," said Magda. "All my good dependable Aryan girls are working in the factories and some of them are doing jobs nearly as dangerous as what they have the foreign workers do. On the streets you see these Slavs walking around, sometimes making eye contact as if they were our equals. Sometimes they even use the sidewalks."

"Scandalous," said Angela. She gestured toward the now-empty cookie plate. "Girl, bring us more sweets."

I could feel my face go bright red as I picked up the plate and took it to the kitchen. Frau Huber filled it with a selection of Linzer cookies and gingersnaps, and I went back out to the dining room. I felt like throwing the plate of cookies at them, but instead I gently set it in the middle of the table and walked out. There were many chores to do, and this was just one of them.

As summer wore on, more women came, and the bunk room filled up completely. Otto moved back upstairs to his old bedroom. "The light still bothers me a little bit," he said as I helped him carry up his things. "But those women, they talk and laugh all night, and that bothers me even more."

Some of the women weren't officers' wives but were bona fide refugees. Frau Huber had us transform the library into a dorm, and then put extra bedding on Sophie's bedroom floor so four people could sleep in there.

With each new arrival, Frau Huber took their ration cards so she could buy more food, but the house was chaotic, and each woman was only interested in her own needs. The farmhouse was bursting with strangers who squabbled among themselves and who took what they wanted without asking.

Once, I found a woman sitting on the front step of the farmhouse playing with her toddler. It would have been like a scene out of a book, except she was wearing a dress she'd taken without asking from Frau Huber's own closet. And the toddler was swaddled in the lace tablecloth that had been on the dining room table! When Frau Huber pointed this out, the woman got angry with her. "My entire house is now rubble," she said. "And you're criticizing me for taking your dress and tablecloth?"

Frau Huber had to put a padlock on the root cellar door because things kept going missing. The final straw was when she found a woman sitting on the bottom step, finishing off an entire jar of apricot preserves with a tablespoon.

It wasn't just Germans who were displaced by the Allied bombings. When factories and concentration camps were destroyed, many forced workers were killed or injured, but others managed to escape, and some fled to our region. From time to time an escaped slave would make it to the Huber farm, and when this happened, Bianka and I would hide them and feed them if we could.

CHAPTER TWENTY
WHAT WE WANT

And then, in July, as I was settling down to sleep in my cow stall after an exhausting day, I heard a soft *kak kak kak* from the loft above.

Had I fallen asleep without knowing it? Surely, I was dreaming that sound. I got up from my willow bed and stepped in front of Bianka's stall. There was enough light streaming in from outside that I could see the startled look in her eyes. She pointed to the loft and whispered, "Did you hear that sound?"

"So you heard it too?" I whispered.

She nodded.

I wasn't dreaming.

"Do you think there's a bat in the loft?" she asked.

That made me smile. "Not likely," I said. "Go back to sleep. I'll go up and see."

"Thank you," she said. And she closed her eyes.

I climbed up the ladder as quickly as I could and when my feet hit the floor of the loft, I squinted to get a better look in the dimness. There he was, my Nathan, leaning against a bale of hay. His face was lined with exhaustion and the knees of his trousers were gone, but he smiled.

I sat down beside him and leaned my shoulder against his. "Hello, old friend," I said.

"I had to see you again," he said "To make sure you were okay. It terrified me to see the way that policeman hauled you off."

"Anna could have told you I was fine," I said.

"She did," said Nathan. "But I had to see you for myself."

I took his hand, then brought it up to my lips and kissed his knuckles. "How did you escape?"

"I had to time it just right," he said. "I slipped away when they took us up to the mountain to excavate rock. But see? I took your advice and got out when I could."

"You didn't take my advice," I said. "You're here, not on your way to Switzerland."

He took both of my hands in his. "I want you to come to Switzerland with me."

My eyes filled with tears. I took a deep breath and tried to respond, but no words came out. In a simpler world, I wouldn't have to choose between my family and my best friend. But in a simpler world, there was no war.

"Maria, you've got to," he said. "It's not safe for you here anymore either. The Allies will be bombing this area too. It's just a matter of time."

His comment got me angry. I pulled my hands away from his. "You can't compare my risk with yours," I said. "You could be executed any second."

"You helped me escape the killing squad in Viteretz," he said. "Now it's my turn to help you."

"Then get out of here," I said in a voice that was between a scream and a whisper. "If you really care for me, you'll get to a neutral country as quickly as you can. Once I know you're safe I'll be able to sleep at night."

"But we're a team," he said. "Practically brother and sister."

"I cannot leave this farm," I said. "Mama and Krystia know I'm here. When the war ends, we need to find each other."

"But my father also thinks I'm here," said Nathan. "So what kind of an argument is that?"

"Do you really think your father would still be in Viteretz?" I asked. "I hope by now he's escaped on his own false papers. Maybe he's already in Switzerland, waiting for you."

Nathan inhaled sharply. "I hope you're right."

He laid his head on my shoulder. I clasped his hands in mine.

We must have fallen asleep like that because the next thing I knew I woke up with a jolt and it was pitch-dark.

"Nathan," I whispered, shaking his shoulder.

"What . . . Where am I?" he asked.

"You need to go."

I stood up and stretched the kinks out of my knees, then felt around the floor until I found our hidden cache of food. I pulled out a potato, an onion, and a hunk of cheese and wrapped it all in a cloth.

"Here," I said to Nathan, thrusting the cloth into his hands. "Do you know the way to the railway tracks from here?"

"I do," he said.

"You should go before it's daylight," I said. "The Blockleiter for this area is very inquisitive. You don't want her to find a Jew in the loft."

He followed me down the ladder, and I watched as he stepped out into the moonlight. He kissed me on the top of my head, then whispered, "I'll let you know when I get there."

And with that, he was gone.

I crawled wearily back into my willow cot but I couldn't

sleep. I tossed and turned, thinking of Nathan escaping in the moonlight. I longed to go with him, to be with my friend.

But we can't have everything that we want.

A Polish girl named Diana took refuge in our barn that summer. I found her cowering in the corner of the empty stall beside my own. "Please don't report me," she said. "They'll send me back to a camp."

"I won't report you," I said, giving her half my bun. "Rest, and get your strength, but don't let the Blockleiter see you."

Diana stayed for more than a week and would even help with the chores sometimes, coming out of hiding once the Blockleiter had visited for the day. "It's just a matter of time before you're caught if you stay," I told her one night as we settled down to sleep.

"But where can I go?" she asked. "I can't go home, and there's war all around us."

I told her about my friend, and about the trains that went through the mountains and ended up in Switzerland. She grinned excitedly.

"I could do that," she said. "I've perfected the technique of riding beneath trains without getting caught."

A day later, she was gone.

Even though the Allies had blasted the Reich with a thousand tons of bombs, they were all on Germany and none on Austria. Frau Lang had a theory about this. "The Allies know we never wanted to be part of the Reich, so they're not bombing us."

But by mid-August, we all knew Frau Lang's theory was just wishful thinking. The Americans bombed a town close to Vienna and destroyed a munitions plant.

"If they can get to Vienna, it's just a matter of time before they'll be able to bomb Innsbruck," said Otto over dinner that night. "We need to build a bomb shelter."

He asked around at neighboring farms and found out that he could rent a group of enslaved construction workers who had already built bomb shelters in the area. They modified the basement of the farmhouse itself by reinforcing the walls and ceiling with steel beams and they made an escape hatch that exited into the garden. It took them about a week.

I thought they would sleep in the barn like we did, but the camp guard that accompanied them insisted they lie out in the open pasture without even a blanket. At least it was summer, and the nights were warm, but I felt so bad for them. The guard also told Frau Huber that she could only give them the same watery turnip soup that they got in camp. "German refugees are starving," he said. "And their needs come first."

But the workers used our outhouse, which was reserved for Slavs, so Frau Huber baked us extra brown buns and we hid them in the outhouse, knowing the guard would never go in the Slav facilities.

It was kind of Frau Huber to give those starving men some extra food, especially because she could end up in a camp herself if she were caught. But this was the same woman who I overheard comparing Slavs to cockroaches. What did she really think of us?

By fall, many escaped slaves had passed through our barn and I began thinking that maybe I should also escape on the route I'd told so many others to take. One thing stopped me though: Mama and Krystia. They knew I was at the Huber farm. If they had to leave Viteretz, they'd come here. If I went to Switzerland, how would I ever find them again?

But then I got the shock of my life. Diana came back to our farm.

"I thought you were going to Switzerland," I said,

sitting her down at our table in the barn and pouring her a glass of water.

"I did," she said. "But they wouldn't let me in. There were huge numbers of refugees. They accepted some, but not all. When it was my turn in line, the border guard said, 'The boat is full.'"

Her statement hit me like a punch. Had Nathan been turned away? I sat down beside Diana and held my head in my hands. Instead of helping, I had made it worse. Were we all trapped in Hitler's web?

Diana slept hidden in the rafters that night, but by morning, she was gone.

CHAPTER TWENTY-ONE
WOMEN'S WORK

Fall arrived and still no bombs had dropped near Innsbruck. Our area was viewed as a haven from war and so refugees kept on coming in wave after wave as cities in the Reich were destroyed. Injured soldiers also came to convalesce in relative safety.

The slave camp system was a frightening invention and it grew like a cancer all over the Ostmark. Seeing chained lines of exhausted prisoners marched at gunpoint from one job to another was an all-too-common experience. My heart ached at the sight of these unfortunates, but it also made me grateful to be on the Huber farm, where I was treated so much better than most. Yet I was acutely aware that all that stood between me and a slave camp was one word from an Aryan.

But over the last few months, I had noticed a change in Frau Huber's attitude toward Slavs, and I think it was partly because of the way the German refugees treated her, assuming they were better than she was and that they could order her around. But what really changed her was seeing the people from the camps. Every time a big job had to be done at the farm, a new group of ragged and starving prisoners would arrive on trucks as if they were nothing more than pieces of a machine.

The frailest prisoners we got were for harvest in late October.

The Blockleiter came into the barn just as Bianka and I were shoveling manure out of the last cow stall. I propped the pitchfork against the wall and stood up straight to greet her. Bianka did the same.

"You're both needed for cooking today," she said. "Three truckloads of prisoners are being sent in to harvest."

Work teams in the past had been a handful of prisoners, six at the most, and making their sorry excuse for soup wasn't a big job.

Bianka looked down at her filthy skirt. "We'll need to get cleaned up first," she said. "Frau Huber won't let us in the kitchen like this."

"You won't be cooking in the kitchen," said the Blockleiter. "Just wash up at the pump and come to the front of the house as soon as you can."

When she was out of earshot, I asked Bianka, "Where do you think they've come from this time?"

"For three truckloads, they have to be fairly close. Maybe the Reichenau Camp in Innsbruck."

There was only a single burlap sack of turnips and another of cabbage sitting on the outdoor table in front of the house when we got there. Three truckloads of prisoners—that would be about thirty men—would be sharing these meager supplies. A firepit had been set up, and Otto was helping his grandfather place a metal grill over the top of it. The Blockleiter stood by, watching.

Frau Huber had placed a large stockpot on the front step, so we each took a handle and lugged it over to the firepit, positioning it on top. Frau Huber was a few steps behind us, carrying a couple of knives and a big wooden spoon.

She placed the utensils on the table, then gestured toward the burlap sacks. "The Blockleiter has arranged for a group of Reichenau prisoners to get the harvest in," she said. "I've been given strict instructions about what they're allowed to eat, so please be obedient in the preparation."

Otto and Herr Lang had finished with setting up the grill, so they walked toward the storage shed. The Blockleiter took a few steps closer to us and seemed to be listening in.

Frau Huber handed us each a knife. "The cabbages and turnips are to be chopped into chunks and all of it goes into the pot. There is to be no peel or root or scrap unused."

The Blockleiter nodded in approval, then went down to the laneway. When she was out of earshot, I whispered, "Will we be adding something to this?"

Frau Huber looked anxiously around. No German refugees were visible, but they could be lurking. Frau Huber looked meaningfully at us and said in a loud voice, "You are to add nothing more to this soup. Just these vegetables and water."

"Yes, Frau Huber," Bianka and I responded together, our voices equally loud.

Before starting on the vegetables, Bianka and I carried pail upon pail of water from the pump out back to fill up the stock pot. Just as we were finishing, a truck came down the laneway and pulled in front of Blockleiter Doris.

The back was crammed with emaciated men. How much work could these poor creatures possibly do? A guard got out of the passenger side and chatted to the Blockleiter for a few moments. She saluted good-bye, then got into her car and drove away.

The guard poised one hand over his gun and the other on a club as he strode to the back of the truck and let down the gate.

"*Aus, aus, aus,*" he shouted, hitting heads and shoulders at random with his club.

This guard seemed more brutal than those we had witnessed before. Perhaps Reichenau operated on nastier terms, or maybe this guard was a nastier person. The men who were strong enough scrambled out, darting away from the club blows. Others seemed to roll out, landing on their hands and knees. Those who were hit fell out awkwardly. One landed on top of a fellow prisoner.

A second truck pulled up and the scene was repeated. And then a third truck appeared. Once the prisoners were all lined up in a row, the guard with the most medals on his collar strode toward Frau Huber. "*Heil* Hitler," he said, saluting. "Where is the man who runs this farm?"

Frau Huber saluted back. "I run the farm."

The guard gave her a pitying smile. "I'm sure you do your part. Where is your husband?"

"The last I heard, Stalingrad," she said.

The guard's eyebrows rose at the mention of Stalingrad. "I hope he returns safely." He shaded his eyes with one hand, searching behind Frau Huber, then turned and looked to the fields. "Isn't your son home on a war injury?" he asked.

Frau Huber's face went bright red. "He's in the shed

with my father, bringing out the harvest equipment, just like I asked him to."

"Thank you," said the guard. "You can busy yourself with your womanly work. I'll go and talk to the men about how to rig the harvesting teams."

As he walked toward the shed, he pointed at us. "Don't let those Poles near my workers."

"They've been given cooking duties today," replied Frau Huber. "They won't be in the fields."

Frau Huber lit a fire under the pot of water, and as it warmed up, I opened the bag of cabbages and began to chop.

Once the fire was licking up the sides of the pot, Frau Huber stood. "I'll be inside doing *women's work* if you need me," she said.

Chopping vegetables at the outdoor table gave us a good vantage point to watch the Reichenau workers, and it brought back memories of when I had first arrived on the Huber farm. One of the workers navigated the horse and plow like Frau Huber had done on that first day, while others were on their hands and knees picking potatoes out of the dirt and placing them into burlap sacks as Bianka and I had done. There was also a second plow in use, but the straps were fastened around the shoulders of one of the men. He pulled and strained but didn't make much progress. "Hey, Frenchie!" shouted the guard, hitting him in the back with the club. "My grandmother could work faster than you."

"Faster, Russian pig!" yelled another guard at one scrawny man trying to dig up potatoes with a shovel. The prisoner cringed, then tried to dig more quickly, but I'm sure he made more mess than progress.

Otto also walked through the fields, and as he approached each prisoner, his words were too quiet for us to hear, but I could see him give a gentle pat on the back now and again. Herr Lang was off to one side in a heated conversation with another of the guards who had accompanied the men. Herr Lang shook his fist and his face turned red. Finally, he turned and walked away. The guard just stood there with an amused look on his face.

Once the vegetables were all chopped up and added to the pot, Bianka and I took turns stirring with the long wooden spoon. With the flames licking up the side of the pot, this was easier said than done. When it was my turn, I got covered with sweat from the effort and nearly set my skirt on fire.

As midday approached, the vegetables had become nothing more than mushy lumps, and I felt sorry for these men, that this was all they were getting. But then Frau

Huber tapped on the kitchen window and gestured for me to come inside. I handed the spoon over to Bianka and went to the house.

The aroma of fresh coffee was in the air and the table was set for the guards' lunch with pork sandwiches made on fluffy white bread. There was a platter of pickles and sausage and cheese and a beautifully frosted chocolate cake for dessert. In case that wasn't enough for them, two loaves of bread fresh from the oven were cooling on a rack on the counter. I thought of those starving prisoners and their disgusting turnip soup. How I would have loved to give the prisoners this food and make the guards eat the soup!

Frau Huber had a long knife in her hand and was wearing a big smile. "Come out to the laundry shed. I've got something to show you."

A large mound of white cubes that looked like cheese covered the mending table. "What is that?" I asked.

"Lard from the pig carcass in cold storage," she said. "*Mutter* and I have cut it into these cubes, so those men can have a decent meal for once."

"What a wonderful idea," I said. "They'll melt right into the soup and the guards won't even know."

Without thinking, I ran to Frau Huber and hugged her. "Thank you," I said. And then I realized what I had done: Slavs were not allowed to touch Aryans. Would she punish me? I let go and tried to back away, but she clung onto me, and I could feel her hot tears on my shoulder.

"I would have cut up more," said Frau Huber. "But these men have been starving for so long that too much extra food could make them sick."

I stayed in that embrace for a minute, maybe longer, and thought of my own mother and how I wished it was *her* warmth enveloping me. But I was also so grateful to be on this farm with this woman who defied Hitler in the small ways that she could.

I took a deep breath and extricated myself from Frau Huber's embrace, then regarded the mound of cubed lard. "How are we going to get this into the soup without the soldiers noticing?" I asked.

"Buckets," said Frau Lang's voice.

I turned and saw her sitting in the corner. I hadn't even noticed her when I had walked in. "What do you mean, buckets?" I asked.

"The soup has boiled down, hasn't it?" she asked.

"It has," I said.

"Instead of adding water to top up the vat, you'll carry buckets of lard to the vat. We'll fill the bucket and put it by the pump. You can let Bianka know."

I looked from mother to daughter and smiled. "This is a good plan," I said.

When I went back outside lugging the first bucket, the biggest challenge was to stop myself from smiling. I dumped the lard cubes in, whispering to Bianka about the plan as I did so.

"Thank you, Maria," she said, passing the long wooden spoon over to me. "The soup needs more *water*, so I'll fill another pail."

The first bucket of lard went into the soup and melted almost imperceptibly, but when Bianka dumped in the second bucket, the surface of the bubbling liquid went slick with oil.

"The soldiers will notice," said Bianka, her brow covered in a layer of soupy sweat and furrowed with concern.

I took the bucket back to the pump where Frau Huber stood waiting. "How does the soup look?" she asked.

"Not good," I said. "It's shiny. I'm sure they'll notice the added fat."

"Maybe we should add some flour?" she asked.

"But won't that go into lumps?"

"You're right," she said, pacing. "I have an idea. Bring the bucket into the kitchen."

I followed her in and set the bucket down on the floor.

She grabbed one of the freshly baked loaves of bread from the cooling rack on the counter and tossed it to me. "Tear it into small pieces and put them in the bucket."

I thought of those starving men and how they would enjoy devouring this beautiful bread just the way it was, but I understood Frau Huber's plan. The white bread would dissolve in the soup and would soak up the fat.

She began breaking the second loaf into pieces and adding it to the bucket as well.

Just then, the front door opened and the sound of men's voices trailed in.

"*Mutter* has made a pot of coffee," said Otto's voice. "Come in and sit . . ."

Frau Huber threw her half loaf into the bucket. "Get rid of it," she whispered.

I grabbed the bucket and ran down the hallway, but as I slipped out the back door, I turned to look. A couple of bread pieces had fallen out of the bucket and landed on the floor. I didn't want to risk going back and picking them up. I could only hope that the soldier wouldn't notice, and if he did, Frau Huber would be able to come up with a story.

When I got outside, I looked out into the field and my heart nearly stopped in horror. The men had finished working and they were already assembling in a long row at the front of the fields for an inspection. Soon, they would be lining up for their soup.

There was no time for ripping up the rest of the bread. I took a deep breath and forced myself to walk slowly to the front of the house, hefting the bucket as if it were heavy with water.

Bianka's eyes widened when she saw the two half loaves of bread sitting on top of torn bread.

I didn't wait for her to argue. I dumped the whole mess in.

The bread pieces quickly got soggy with soup, while the two half loaves bobbed on the surface.

"This is a disaster," whispered Bianka. "They're going to be here any minute. What's the punishment for giving camp prisoners too much food?"

"Shhh," I said, grabbing the long wooden spoon from her and stirring frantically. The ripped pieces were slowly dissolving and some of them sank, but the surface still glistened with grease.

Bianka ran to the table and got both knives. As I stirred, she impaled one of the loaf halves and hacked it apart. Hunks broke off and swirled and bubbled. Once the first hunk finally disappeared, she attacked the second half loaf. Because it had been in the hot soup longer, it had already soaked up a lot of the liquid, and miraculously, because it had been bobbing along on the top, it had managed to skim off some of the most obvious slicks of grease. By the time it sank down, the bubbling mass looked nearly like just water, turnip, and cabbage.

I hadn't realized until the men lined up that they wore their metal bowls. Some had them on strings around their necks while others had them tucked inside their shirts. Spoons were kept in similarly protective ways. I guess when you're starving, you cherish the implements that hold your food.

A guard came up to the pot. "You girls can go," he said. "I will serve the soup."

Just then, Frau Huber stepped out of the house, holding two large soup ladles. "Officer," she said. "There's coffee inside, freshly brewed, and I've got cream and sugar as well."

"*Real* coffee and sugar?" he asked.

"Yes," she said. "I've saved it for a special occasion. There's also chocolate cake and roast pork sandwiches on fresh white bread. The others have already started to eat and they seem very hungry. I wouldn't want you to miss out."

The guard hesitated. "These Poles are not to fraternize with my men."

"I'll stay out here and supervise," she said, handing each of us a ladle. "You've been doing *men's* work, and you need a break."

"Good point," he said. "It has been hard work, keeping these prisoners in line. I'll go inside."

Once the door had closed behind him, I felt almost faint with relief. We filled the men's soup bowls one by one, and by the expressions on the men's faces, it was obvious even from the sound of the soup hitting their bowls that it contained something more than cabbage and turnip. They held their bowls like precious jewels and each man found a place on the ground to sit and savor the concoction.

We were nearly at the end of the lineup when Bianka clutched my arm. "Lord help me," she said.

"What's the matter?" I asked.

She pointed to the very last prisoner. He had a triangle on his shirt with the letter F. His cheeks were hollow, but his eyebrows were thick and he had an angular nose. Where had I seen that face before?

"That's Gustave," she said.

Frau Huber also recognized her old worker even though he was thin and dirty and had a bruise on the side of his face. She stepped over and took Bianka's ladle. A cluster of prisoners gathered around Gustave and Bianka so that anyone looking from the kitchen window would only notice the prisoners, not Bianka talking to one of them.

They spoke in French in urgent whispers and I had no idea what they said, but the conversation was over in less than a minute. Gustave sat under a tree and ate his soup while Bianka came back to the vat. With a trembling hand, she took the ladle from Frau Huber.

After lunch, we lugged the huge pot to the pump out back and washed it, then cleaned the remnants of the guards' festive lunch. We couldn't watch the workers in the afternoon because Frau Huber sent us to do the laundry.

That night, as we lay down in our willow twig beds in our cow stalls, I said to Bianka, "At least he is alive."

"I can't talk about it," she said. A little bit later, I could hear her sobbing into her pillow.

The next morning when I awoke, Bianka was gone.

The camp guards came back and ransacked the farm, looking for Gustave, but there was no sign of him, and no sign of Bianka.

CHAPTER TWENTY-TWO
THE SAFEST PLACE

I missed Bianka terribly, but her Gustave was alive, and they had escaped together. With all the refugees on the move, both Aryan and foreign, now was the perfect time to leave and blend in. I dreamed of tearing off my letter P and leaving.

But I couldn't do that.

How would Mama and Krystia ever find me if I left this farm?

Nathan—

Had he been turned away at the border, or was he safe? I'd had no word from him. But then again, how would he get word to me?

The weeks sped by in a blur of work, and it wasn't easy being the only foreign worker who still lived on the Huber farm. I would have felt lonely had it not been for the steady stream of foreign workers who took refuge in the barn.

Out of desperation, Frau Huber allowed them to stay for a few days or even a week in exchange for helping me with the chores. Even Blockleiter Doris turned a blind eye to this, because if she didn't, how would she collect the quota of milk and eggs and produce from the Huber farm?

Aryan refugees took over the house, stealing the bedding and furniture, breaking dishes, taking clothing and linens without asking. Frau Huber and her family were cramped into a single bedroom, living one day at a time.

The only glimmer of hope was that we had not been bombed.

But then in the wee hours of December 15, 1943, the day after my thirteenth birthday, I woke to the sound of planes overhead and a high-pitched whistling sound. I ran outside and looked in the sky. Toward Innsbruck, there was a burst of smoke, then fire. The bombs were terrifyingly close.

Once it was daylight and the bombing had stopped, some of those injured were brought to Thaur, so I went with Frau Huber and her parents into town to bandage and feed and assist in any way that I could.

Four days later, there was a second air strike, but this time Frau Huber heard it on the radio. She went outside and banged on her pot, ordering everyone into the air shelter.

Everyone, that is, except me.

I stood in line with the others, but an Aryan refugee blocked my way. "Slavs are not allowed," she said, closing the door in my face. What hurt even more was that no one in the Huber family came to my defense.

It was terrifying, watching a battle of warplanes above my head, knowing that a bomb could drop down at any moment and I'd be dead. At first, I could barely breathe, waiting for the worst to happen, but as the battle above me played out, a sense of calm settled over me. If Mama were here, she'd tell me that there was no point in worrying about the bombs. Worrying wouldn't change the future, it would just ruin today. As the bombs exploded overhead, I thought about the gift of solitude that I had just been given. No one was ordering me around. For once, I was my own boss. Max came out of nowhere and bounded up beside me, jumping up and nearly knocking me over, he was so grateful for company. I buried my face in his fur, taking comfort in his warmth. A loud boom, and the ground shook—a very close bomb. I stood up and Max looked at me expectantly. "Let's go to the house," I said.

The place was in shambles, with dirty plates and half-eaten meals scattered around the kitchen and into the dining room. There were muddy footprints making a path from one room to another and someone had draped a men's winter jacket over the opened door of the oven to dry. Amid the debris on the kitchen table sat the wireless radio, but now it was transmitting only static. I rinsed off a dirty glass and filled it with milk from the icebox and brought it back to the table with me. Max sat beside the table, looking at me with hopeful eyes, so I found a part of a meat sandwich and put it on the floor for him to eat. I fiddled with the radio dials but couldn't find a channel. Max had finished off his sandwich with a single gulp, so I drank down my milk, cleaned the glass, dried it, and put it in the cupboard: It was the only glass there.

I walked back toward the barn with Max by my side. None of the chickens were pecking for seeds. Were they afraid of bombs as well? I grabbed a handful of corn and stuck my head in through the door of the coop. All were like statues on their nests and all eyes turned toward me. "It will be over soon," I said in as soothing a tone as I could manage, scattering the corn on the floor of the coop.

When Max and I got to the barn, the cows were eerily silent and still as well. It hadn't occurred to me that cows ever worried. It certainly seemed that they were worrying about the warplanes overhead. I filled up their water troughs and gave them each a bit of feed. It wasn't the usual time to be feeding them, but an extra snack might calm them.

That entire winter, the bombs kept on falling, and while the buildings of Innsbruck were blasted to rubble, our farm wasn't touched. I knew that could change, but I lived in the moment, determined to relish my time with the cows, the chickens, and Max. I was alive, I was not starving, and Frau Huber was kinder than expected.

In late March, Frau Huber came out to the barn one evening and she sat at my table, then patted the stool beside her, saying, "Sit down, Maria, we need to talk."

I sat down, my heart bounding. "Did I do something wrong?" I asked. Was I about to be sent to a work camp?

"You've always been reliable," said Frau Huber. "It's not that at all."

She pulled an envelope from her pocket and set it in front of me. It was addressed to her, but there was no return address. The postage stamp was from Switzerland. She tapped the stamp with her index finger and said, "I don't know anyone in Switzerland. Do you?"

I could barely think or speak, so I shrugged. "Have you opened it?" I asked.

"I did," she said. "But it doesn't make sense."

"I . . . would . . . maybe I could help . . . ?"

She handed me the envelope. I opened it with trembling fingers:

Falcon is free

Nathan was free. He had made it through the Swiss border somehow. He was safe. I felt like laughing, like dancing for joy. If Bianka were still here, we would have done a polka around the cow barn. But could I share this good news with Frau Huber? Probably, but I couldn't be sure. I took a deep breath in and let it out slowly so that my heart would stop pounding, and I did my best to keep my face from smiling.

"I'm not sure what that means," I said.

She took the letter from my hand and put it back into the envelope. "Thanks for looking at it," she said. "Otto thought you might be able to figure it out; I don't know why."

After she left the barn, I cradled my head in my arms and wept for joy.

CHAPTER TWENTY-THREE
TWO HIDING IN PLAIN SIGHT

I was living in the midst of chaos, yet I could barely contain my sense of optimism.

Nathan was safe.

The war had to be nearly over.

Soon I could go home.

Soon I would be with Mama and Krystia.

But spring turned to summer, then fall, and the war didn't end.

During an air raid in December 1944, while I sat wrapped in a blanket at the outdoor table with Max by my side, I spied a girl in trousers and jacket walking up the laneway. The tilt of her head, her determined gait. My heart stood still. Could it be Krystia? But how could it be just Krystia? She would never have left Mama behind. I got up and walked toward her, Max a few steps behind me. I turned to him and said, "Stay," knowing that if this girl was my sister, she'd be afraid of Max, just like I used to be.

Max looked at me with plaintive eyes, but he was still, except for his tail thumping in the snow. I walked down the lane to meet the girl.

It was Krystia. Just Krystia. Not Mama and Krystia.

I grabbed her shoulders. "Where's Mama?"

Her eyes filled with tears and her mouth opened, but no words came out.

I shook her by the shoulders. "Tell me," I screamed.

"Mama is dead."

"But you were supposed to protect her."

"That's not fair," she said. "I'm just one girl. I did what I could. Maybe if you'd stayed, you could have helped me."

I hit her hard in the shoulder and her knees buckled. She fell to the snow. I watched as she curled up and wept.

"I'm sorry," she said. "I did what I thought was right, but I couldn't save her."

I took a deep breath and let it out slowly. My sister was the bravest person I knew. That is, except for Mama. If anyone could have saved Mama, it would have been Krystia.

I collapsed beside her in the dirt and gathered her to me.

"I'm sorry," I said. "It couldn't have been your fault. Tell me what happened."

It took a while for her to catch her breath from the gasping sobs, but finally she whispered, "Nathan's father came to us. He asked us to hide him."

My heart stopped beating. I should have known. I thought of Bianka and Debora. Bianka hesitated, and Debora died. My sister would not hesitate. Nor would Mama.

"And you said yes."

"Of course. Uncle Ivan helped us dig a hole in the kitchen floor, beneath the stove."

"Under the metal plate?"

"Yes."

It was a smart hiding place. An image formed in my mind: Krystia getting rid of dirt a teaspoon at a time so the Nazis wouldn't know a hole was being dug. Mama continuing to work for the Commandant so he wouldn't suspect her duplicity. Had I stayed, I would have helped.

"How long did he hide there?"

"It wasn't just him," said Krystia. "I asked Mama to hide Dolik and Leon as well."

Ukrainians hiding Jews. That was like the doomed hiding the more doomed. But Dolik was Krystia's special friend and also our next-door neighbor. Leon was his little brother. And Nathan's father, Mr. Segal? He was one of Mama's oldest friends. How could they say no?

"The Commandant found out?" I asked.

Krystia took a deep shuddering breath. "Not for a long time," she said. "We thought we had fooled him, but Marga saw the extra water we took to our house and the extra slop pails that went to the privy. She told the Commandant."

My fists clenched in anger.

Marga.

The Hitler Girl who tormented Krystia like Sophie tormented me.

I propped myself up on one elbow and gazed into my sister's tortured face. "How did Mama die?"

Krystia didn't answer for the longest time. Finally, she whispered, "Hanged. In the town square."

I gasped. An image formed in my mind. Mama swinging lifeless from a noose. I wished I hadn't asked. But then again, I had to know.

"What happened to Dolik, Leon, and Nathan's father?"

"You know what happened," she said. "Do I really need to tell you?"

"Shot into a pit in the woods?"

Krystia's eyes were closed but she nodded, tears streaming down her face. "I tried to stop the Commandant," she said. "But when I got to the killing pit, it was already too late."

Nathan's father had not been able to use his false papers. He wouldn't be waiting for Nathan in Switzerland.

Mama dead.

Mr. Segal dead.

Dolik and Leon dead.

I stayed there in the dirt and grieved with my sister. The enormity of all that we had lost had stunned us into silence. Our arms wrapped around each other and we wept, while above us bombs exploded and Allied planes flew by.

It was Max who finally broke the spell. He edged closer to us, whimpering almost imperceptibly at first, but then with more urgency. He nuzzled at my sleeve, then licked my face, and licked Krystia's too. That jolted her and she sat up.

"What is that dog doing here?" she said, pushing Max away.

"It's okay," I said. "He's friendly. Let him smell you."

Krystia held her palm out to Max so he could sniff it.

He sniffed her hand, then licked her face, then pinned her to the ground and licked her some more. As he did that, he howled with such a sorrow that it made her almost smile.

I pulled Max off her and she stood up. I got up too. She and I and Max walked to the barn together.

I poured her some water and found a potato for us to share and we sat side by side in our silence and sorrow, with Max hovering near.

I forced myself to take a sip of water, then said, "I am so glad that you found me."

Krystia reached out and squeezed my hand. "The last thing Mama told me was that I had to find you," she said. "I'm so glad that you stayed on this farm."

That night we lay side by side on my narrow willow cot in the cow stall with Max at our feet. Krystia held me and rocked me like Mama used to do.

"After the Commandant killed Mama, he kicked me out of our house."

"Where did you go?" I asked.

"Anya, the priest's wife, took me in. She would have let me stay, but knowing the Commandant, she would have been punished for helping me, so I escaped to the woods."

"To Auntie Iryna and Uncle Ivan?"

"Yes," she said. "And the Underground Army. Auntie Iryna nursed me back to health and she taught me how to survive on my own. But much as I wanted to find you, I stayed in the woods and helped fight the Nazis. The

Soviets arrived this summer, and as the Nazis fled, I couldn't wait any longer. I started on my journey—to you."

I hugged her fiercely and I wept. When I was finally able to catch my breath, I told her about Nathan, how we were separated, and how he was safe now in Switzerland.

"Of all our Jewish friends, only Nathan has survived," whispered Krystia. "And that's because you helped him. You, my brave dear sister."

We hugged each other in sadness and silence, and somehow fell asleep. When it was daylight, we walked out of the barn and together stood in the middle of the potato field. "It's our time to get out," she said, pointing to the sky. "See the warplanes? When they're fighting, we're the safest. The Aryans are all cowering in their bomb shelters. That's how I got to this farm, traveling while the Aryans hid."

"Are we going back to Viteretz?" I asked her.

"With Mama dead and our house confiscated, Viteretz just has bad memories," she said.

"Then where will we go?" I asked.

"When the war is over, we'll go to Auntie Stefa's," she said. "In the meantime, we'll hide and survive."

I thought of that photograph, of the woman who looked so much like Mama, only untouched by war. "Do you think Auntie Stefa will still want us to join her in Canada?" I asked.

"I know she will," said Krystia.

Mama would have wanted this. That I knew for sure.

When my sister and I stood in front of Frau Huber, they eyed each other solemnly.

"I suppose you're leaving me now, Maria," said Frau Huber.

"I need to be with my sister," I replied. "And we need to get away from here."

She ran upstairs, coming back moments later with my identification papers. It felt so good to finally have them back. She packed us each a rucksack with bread and cheese and even gave us a few coins each.

She wrapped her arms around my shoulders and gave me a tight squeeze. "You've been almost like a daughter to me," she said.

How could I respond to that? A daughter would have been let inside the bomb shelter. A daughter wouldn't have to sleep in the barn or nearly starve. But I was lucky, landing on this farm. "Thank you for your kindness," I said, and I meant it.

"Stay safe," said Frau Huber. "And if you decide to come back, you're welcome here. Your sister too."

I said good-bye to the chickens and kissed each cow on the bridge of its nose. I found it hardest to say good-bye to Max as I crouched down one last time and wrapped my arms around his warm neck, whispering in his ear, "I'll miss you, old friend."

Krystia and I walked at the base of the foothills, staying off the roads and railway lines but keeping them in our sight. As the days and weeks wore on, the roads and railway tracks became congested as more people fled the war zone. Women with babies, men on crutches, some speaking languages I had never heard before. But most of what we saw were people like us, dressed in rags, bone-frail, with a P or OST sewn on their clothing. We followed them, but we didn't let them see us. And I wore my own coat inside out so the P didn't show.

Once, we stayed hidden behind bushes as a cluster of refugees we were following arrived at a war-damaged town. Four exhausted-looking Nazi soldiers got out of an idling truck and positioned themselves to block the road and drew their guns.

"Stop and turn back!" shouted the one who seemed to be in charge.

Most of the people in the group stopped, but no one turned around. A thin woman wearing a black shawl over her hair stepped forward. "We have no place to turn back to," she said. "You may as well let us go through."

As if on cue, all four soldiers pointed their guns at the woman's head. "One step closer and we shoot."

The woman turned toward the civilian group and said, "We either die going back or die going forward, so I'm going forward."

Krystia tugged me deeper into the bushes. She wrapped an arm around my waist and we both closed our eyes, praying that the soldiers would let the others pass.

Gun blasts pierced the air and I nearly cried out loud, but Krystia clamped her hand over my mouth. I was so filled with sorrow that I couldn't stop shaking.

Krystia hugged me and we wept in silence, staying hidden as the soldiers dragged the bodies away. For me, and I'm sure for Krystia too, hearing what happened was almost like having Mama killed again. We waited until the soldiers left, then crept out from behind the bushes. I couldn't bury Mama, and I couldn't bury these victims, but I could give these brave people some dignity in death. I gathered a handful of dirt, and so did Krystia.

We sprinkled it over their dusty footsteps in the road, whispered a quick prayer, then hid again. I wanted to sing the *Vichnaya Pamyat*—"Eternal Memory"—for these dead souls but we couldn't risk the soldiers coming back. We stayed hidden in the bushes all that night, saying our silent prayers. The next day, there was an air raid, and while war planes dropped bombs above us, Krystia and I sang the *Vichnaya Pamyat*. As I sang, I remembered Mama.

I wish I could say that massacre was a solitary incident, but it wasn't. We saw similar incidents with sad regularity. The Nazis didn't see the survivors fleeing as victims but as witnesses to their own misdeeds. And they wanted to pretend their misdeeds never happened.

CHAPTER TWENTY-FOUR
HITLER IS DEAD

Days had gone by with no bombs dropping from the sky. Rumors swirled that Hitler was dead and the war would soon be over.

The refugees traveled out in the open, walking in clusters along the roads, but Krystia and I still stayed hidden, darting from one pile of rubble to the next, keeping the other refugees in sight.

The war did seem to be waning but there was still danger. More than once, an impossibly young Nazi soldier would burst out of nowhere and shoot wildly into the crowd of refugees. There couldn't have been too many Nazi soldiers left, what with Hitler dead, but there were still some Nazis out there who thought they could win.

From our hiding spots, bits of conversation would drift back to us and that's how we heard rumor that it wasn't just the *Nazi* soldiers that had to be avoided. Soviet soldiers were bad in different ways.

They attacked women and girls, refugee and German alike.

Would we be safer from these Soviet soldiers if we traveled in a group, or was it better to hide and travel alone like we had been? For now, even though it was hard walking through the brush and rubble on shredded shoes, we continued to hide.

As days passed, the sound of war gradually subsided, and in its place was what sounded like leaves rustling in the wind—only there were no leaves. What we heard was rag-covered feet mechanically shuffling forward. Hundreds of thousands of rag-covered feet. Who could have guessed that shuffling could be so loud?

When night came, this entire mass of humanity collapsed as one, lying in the road to sleep. The shuffling was replaced with exhausted sighs and sobs and whispers. Each day, another dozen or fifty bedraggled people joined the exodus.

One morning I woke to the warbling song of a finch. The sound gave me hope. Maybe things would get better. Maybe the war was well and truly over.

Krystia sat up beside me, rubbing the sleep out of her

eyes. She tilted her head at the sound of the birdsong and smiled. "Let's walk on the road with everyone else."

I didn't answer her right away. What would Mama have wanted us to do? We were sure to encounter Soviets soon. They were allied with the British and Americans, after all. Would we be safer hiding, or in a crowd? It was hard to know for sure. But if Krystia wanted to walk with the crowd, that's where I wanted to be as well. She was my sister and we'd stick together.

We stepped out of the bushes and scrambled down to the road, stepping in among the river of refugees, clasping hands so we wouldn't lose each other in the crush of people.

Now that we were walking among the others, I saw each person as an individual. I tried not to stare at the one-legged man in front of me who used a broken shovel as a crutch. Beside Krystia was a solemn mother who introduced herself to us as Dasha; she carried the corpse of baby Anna strapped to her shoulders. To the right of me a bent old woman and a tiny skeletal child shuffled along as if in a trance. My heart filled with anger. All this misery, and why? Because two madmen—Hitler and Stalin—saw countries and humans as nothing more than toys they could play with.

That first night when we slept on the road with

everyone else, I woke up with a jolt to a terrible itchy squirming on my legs and arms. Scratching only made it worse and I tossed and turned all night. The next morning, there were red dots all over my skin. A woman who was just waking up beside me said, "Lice. You'd better get used to them. With all of us walking together like this, we all have them."

During the daytime as we walked, I was able to put the itchiness out of my mind, but at night it was nearly impossible. I could feel the little bugs on my scalp and in my armpits. And the red raised patches of infected bites on my arms and legs were hard to ignore.

Krystia was covered in red bites too, especially her neck and the backs of her knees, but she was stoic about it all. "At least these bugs don't have guns," she said with a smile. "I can put up with these creatures if it means we get to somewhere safe."

With so many people walking as one, finding food was nearly impossible. The fields had been picked clean. Even spring shoots of grass and wildflowers had been eaten down to the root. I think Krystia and I lived on gulps of water. We made a point of cupping our hands in any stream or river that wasn't clogged with bloating corpses, but they were few and far between. Besides, no amount of water could stave off the gnawing ache of an empty belly.

While most of those traveling with us were as ragged and tired as we were, every once in a while I would notice a refugee who seemed out of place: clothing that looked too new, or cheeks that weren't hollow. Once, I saw a woman in a smart blue dress, her blond hair pulled back in a bun. My heart skipped double. She looked like that Nazi nurse in Viteretz who only helped German patients. It couldn't be. She wasn't a refugee, was she? But as I looked around, there were others who were also too well off to be victims. I got angry all over again, thinking of perpetrators hiding as victims.

Suddenly, those in front of us stopped. I would have walked right into the man with the shovel crutch if Krystia hadn't grabbed my arm and steadied me.

"What's happening?" she asked, arching her neck and trying to peer between the shoulders of those in front of us.

We moved a few footsteps in the next hour, and then a few footsteps more. It took a day to edge closer to whatever was blocking our group. Finally, as the sun was setting, an encampment of some sort came into view.

"I see tents and trucks up ahead," I told Krystia.

A woman a few meters in front of us turned and said, "They're soldiers, but they just raised an *American* flag."

American soldiers? Not Soviet, not Nazi. This was promising.

More excited chatter rippled down the ribbon of refugees and Dasha turned. Her eyes were bright with hope. "They are giving out *food* once you get inside the camp."

"A camp?" Krystia smiled. "Maybe we're finally safe."

We slept in place on the road that night, but early the next morning when I stood on my toes, I could see tents in a row and an American flag.

As we got closer to the front of the lineup, we both had a clearer idea of what was going on. People would enter one of the canvas tents, but they didn't come out again.

When it was finally our turn, I clutched Krystia's hand and we stepped in front of the row of tents. The flap of the nearest tent parted, and a woman's voice said something in a language I didn't understand. She tried again in a different language, but still not one that we knew. Next, she tried German: *"Bitte komm,"* which means "come in," so we stepped inside.

She pulled the tent flaps securely shut and my nose wrinkled at an odor that was something like petroleum. The woman wore a long-sleeved shirt and men's trousers, and her face was mostly covered with a scarf, but her eyes looked friendly. In one arm, she cradled an instrument that looked something like a long gun.

She must have noted the alarm on my face because she aimed the instrument above my head and pulled on the handle. A powdery smoke puffed out of the muzzle instead of a bullet. I exhaled with relief.

She motioned for us to stand side by side with our eyes closed and arms raised above our heads. She sprayed our hair slowly and methodically, making sure that every strand got covered with the powdery chemical. She sprayed our clothing and legs and arms as well. By the time she was finished, I was afraid to breathe. I shook my head vigorously to get the powder out of my eyes and nostrils. My lungs were burning. I opened my eyes.

On the ground around me and Krystia were dozens of dead bugs. That powder had to be a lethal poison to work so quickly. I ran my fingers through my hair, and more bugs fell to the ground.

The woman said, *"Alles erledig"*—all done. Then she opened a flap on the other side of the tent and walked toward it, motioning for us to follow her.

Even though my lungs felt like they would explode, I didn't take a gulp of air until we were outside the tent. If that chemical powder killed bugs so quickly, I couldn't imagine that it would be good for our lungs.

Now that we were beyond the barrier of the canvas tents, we faced a row of men in uniform sitting at folding tables, sorting through stacks of papers.

Refugees coated in the white powder stood before them.

When we were at the front, a soldier came over to us. *"Welche Nationalität hast du?"* he asked in German. What nationality are you?

"Ukrainian," I said, pointing to me and then my sister.

The soldier held up one finger and nodded, then left. A few moments later, a different soldier approached us. "You're Ukrainian?" he asked—in Ukrainian!

I squeezed Krystia's hand. "We are," I said.

"Ukrainians register over there," he said, pointing.

"What happens when we register?" I asked.

"We stamp your papers to show you've been registered, then give you food and a place to sleep," said the soldier.

CHAPTER TWENTY-FIVE
FAMILY

We walked up to the desk. The man looked at my face, then Krystia's. He smiled, and said in Ukrainian, "Are you sisters?"

"We are," I said.

"Do you have identification?"

I reached into my pocket and handed it to him.

The soldier flattened both of my papers on his desk and examined them carefully. Then he looked into my eyes and said, "What did you do during the war?"

I looked down at the form he was filling out and saw that he only wanted a bit of information. Just enough to write inside a small square box the size of a postage stamp. How could the sum of my war experiences be reduced to that? Should I tell him about my escape with Nathan? Or Mama being hanged? Or would he be more interested in the fact that I volunteered to milk cows to feed Nazi soldiers?

The soldier drummed his fingers on his desk. "Let me make this easy for you," he said. "Did you work in a German factory or a farm?"

"A farm, but in Austria," I said.

"Ah," said the soldier. He inserted "forced farm labor" in the small square, stamped my card, and handed it back.

He interviewed Krystia next and stamped her identification papers too.

"Are you planning on going back to Viteretz once it's safe to do so?" he asked, looking from Krystia to me.

I took a deep breath and thought of Mama. Didn't he realize how painful that question was? "There's no one to go back to," I replied.

He set down his pen and sighed. "Do you know of any surviving relatives?"

I couldn't tell him about my aunt and uncle still hiding in the woods near Viteretz with their fellow insurgents, because now with the Nazis gone, they were fighting back the Soviets—and the Americans wouldn't understand that the Soviets were our enemies just like the Nazis were.

I didn't know what to say. He threw his pen on the table. "You're holding up the line," he said.

"Our Auntie Stefa Pidhirney," Krystia piped in. "She lives in Canada."

The soldier's face relaxed. "That's good," he said, picking up his pen again. He grabbed a form from a different pile. "Do you know where, in Canada?" He poised the pen above the new form.

"We haven't heard from her since the war began," I said. "But she used to send us packages. They came from an address in Toronto."

"On Franklin Street in Toronto," said Krystia.

The soldier's eyes lit up. "There's an old Ukrainian church on that street. My Canadian cousins live around the corner. You can both go through," he said. "Once you've had something to eat and found a place to sleep, go to the tent marked with the red cross. They'll help you fill out paperwork to find your aunt."

The weight of the world lifted from my shoulders. Mama would be so happy. "Thank you," I said, my voice hoarse with tears.

I clutched Krystia's hand in mine and together we strode past the armored trucks and through to the enclosure area beyond.

AUTHOR'S NOTE

MARIA AND NATHAN'S stories are inspired by real events in World War II.

If you look at a map of Eastern Europe in World War II, you'll see that what is now Poland and Ukraine was squeezed between Nazi Germany and the Soviet Union. The fiercest battles in Europe were fought between the Soviets and Nazis on these lands. For those who lived in this war zone, it was a treacherous time.

The Nazis intended to empty the area of the people who had lived there for centuries. Hitler wanted this land as *Lebensraum* or "living space" for Germans, whom he considered to be superior humans. Most Jews were either shot or gassed to death. Those labeled "Slavs" (Poles, Ukrainians, Czechs) were to be starved and worked to death. Hitler intended to kill thirty million Slavs and Jews. As Jews were killed or taken away, Aryans (people of Germanic or Nordic heritage) were brought in by the Nazis to replace them. All able-bodied Aryan German males were drafted into the

German army, and this created an employment crisis in the German Reich. To solve the crisis, the Nazis wanted laborers from Poland and Ukraine for factories and farms and munitions plants. Early in the war, the Germans circulated advertisements, enticing Eastern Europeans to sign up for work in Germany, promising payment and food. Generations of Eastern Europeans had been traveling to Western Europe as migrant workers and so this didn't seem unusual. A small number of people did sign up, but they quickly realized that the ads were lies. They were not paid, and they were barely fed. Word soon trickled back that this was slavery, not employment, so people stopped going.

Nazis still needed workers, though, so they kidnapped people and brought them to the Reich by force, where they were brutally worked and starved, sometimes to death. The slave workers captured from what is now Poland and western Ukraine were forced to wear the letter P on their clothing to identify them as Polish slave workers. Those from what is now Eastern Ukraine were forced to wear OST on their clothing, to identify them as *Ostarbeiters*, or slave workers from the east. In my novel *Making Bombs for Hitler*, I write about Lida, a captured *Ostarbeiter*.

Living as a slave worker was horrible, but for some people living in the war zone, escaping into the Reich for slave labor offered a slim chance of survival. For Nathan, who was Jewish, the alternative would have been death. Maria chose to go with him, thinking she could help.

Trapped in Hitler's Web is a deeply personal story for me: My husband's father, the late Dr. John Skrypuch (whom I called Tusio—an affectionate Ukrainian term for "father"), lived in a town not far from Maria and Nathan's.

Like them, he slipped into the Reich in the hopes of survival.

In 1941, John was a nineteen-year-old medical student who had miraculously evaded execution by the Soviets— but just as they fled, the Nazis arrived. This was the second army that invaded John's town in two years. He had wanted nothing to do with the Soviets and he wanted nothing to do with the Nazis. He escaped from the war zone by hopping on a train going into the Reich, hiding as a farmworker. The last time John saw his mother was when she passed him a package of *nalysnyky* (crepes) through the train window as it chugged away. John hid out in rural Germany throughout the war, doing heavy labor on remote farms. When he finally got to a refugee camp at the end of the war, he was emaciated and sick, and he nearly died of typhus. As I wrote and researched Maria and Nathan's stories, I kept on thinking about my gentle father-in-law.

While doing research for this book, I delved deeply into to the day-to-day life of Austrian civilians during the war.

This was a chilling exploration of how a seemingly civilized society could transform itself into something utterly evil.

What bothered me the most was that Nazism transformed into a youth movement. By age ten, German boys were required to join the Hitler Youth and German girls were required to join the League of German Girls. They were given better food, more privileges and freedom than their parents and grandparents. They were brainwashed into forgetting that all humans are equal. Instead they were taught that they were special, and that they could judge others. Most of these young people were impressionable enough that they embraced the Nazi way of life. They were a huge part of Hitler's web, committing violence on Jews and Slavs, spying and reporting on their friends and even on their own family members. Sometimes, they got people killed.

One reason that the brainwashing worked back then is because the Nazis burned the books that they didn't like. They knew the power of reading, that the more books you read, the better you could think for yourself. Reading opens up the door to empathy, letting each of us walk in the shoes of someone else and letting us feel what it's like to be them. I can't think of a more powerful tool for creating good—and for making sure that history doesn't repeat itself—than discovering empathy through books.

ACKNOWLEDGMENTS

I AM EXTREMELY grateful to the people at Scholastic Canada, Scholastic Inc., and Scholastic Book Fairs for enabling me to write my stories and for getting my books into the hands of readers.

To my longtime agent, Dean Cooke, thank you for your ongoing expertise and doggedness. Sarah Harvey, it was awesome doing the edits with you. Thank you, Diane Kerner, for your guidance and support over so many books and stories. And Maral Maclagan, you have the golden touch. Aimee Friedman, thank you for encouraging me to write this novel and for your insightful suggestions. Olivia Valcarce, thank you for your keen eye to detail. Thank you, Raya Shadursky and Natalia Feduschak of the Ukrainian Jewish Encounter for helping me to connect with so many varied people and their stories. Thank you, Iryna Korpan, for all your time and expertise and for sharing your heart-breaking family story with me. As always, thank you Orest, my husband, for your patience and love.

Read more about Krystia's story in

DON'T TELL THE NAZIS

by MARSHA FORCHUK SKRYPUCH

A novel by **MARSHA FORCHUK SKRYPUCH**
Author of MAKING BOMBS FOR HITLER

DON'T TELL THE NAZIS

ABOUT THE AUTHOR

MARSHA FORCHUK SKRYPUCH is a Ukrainian Canadian author acclaimed for her nonfiction and historical fiction, including *Making Bombs for Hitler*, *The War Below*, *Stolen Girl*, and *Don't Tell the Nazis*. She was awarded the Order of Princess Olha by the president of Ukraine for her writing. Marsha lives in Brantford, Ontario, and you can visit her online at calla.com.